Scottish
Bakehouse
Mysteries™

If Looks Could Kilt

Elizabeth Penney

Annie's®

AnniesFiction.com

Books in the Scottish Bakehouse Mysteries series

The Jig Is Up

If Looks Could Kilt

A Reel Threat

Lass and Found

Silence of the Clans

Shepherd's Lie

A Faerie Dangerous Game

Tartan Feathered

Yule Be Sorry

Of Ice and Men

Reign of Terrier

Aye for an Aye

From Plaid to Worse

Quill the Messenger

Under Loch and Key

Paying the Piper

Isle and Tribulation

Scone Cold Murder

A Hopeless Ness

Settling Auld Scores

A Lass Resort

Heid and Seek

In Grave Danger

Wed on Arrival

If Looks Could Kilt
Copyright © 2020, 2021 Annie's.

Library of Congress-in-Publication Data
If Looks Could Kilt / by Elizabeth Penney
p. cm.
I. Title
                    2019951565

AnniesFiction.com
(800) 282-6643
Scottish Bakehouse Mysteries™
Series Creator: Shari Lohner
Series Editor: Elizabeth Morrissey
Cover Illustrator: Kelley McMorris

10 11 12 13 14 | Printed in China | 9 8 7 6 5 4 3

A drifting mist shrouded the green hills and gathered in the steep valleys below. In the cramped back seat of the rental car, Laura Donovan hugged herself, both against the damp air and in excitement. *I'm in Scotland!* she thought gleefully. *And I'm going to meet my idol!*

Former professional chef Laura and her fellow bakery co-owners, Carol MacCallan and Molly Ferris, had traveled from their home in Scottish-influenced Loch Mallaig, Michigan, to the real Scotland for a workshop taught by celebrity baker Agnes McVie. As if that wasn't enough to send any culinary-minded woman into a tizzy, the master-level class was being held at Glenellen Castle, an ancient estate on the shores of a loch. They hoped to learn new techniques to use in their bakehouse, Bread on Arrival.

"You all right back there?" Molly asked. She sat up front, next to Carol, who had become their designated driver after revealing she'd driven in the United Kingdom before. Under other circumstances, adventurous Laura might have given driving on the left a chance, but having barely slept on their overnight flight, she'd thought it best to wait on that particular new experience. Her brain felt as if it were stuffed with the fog swirling past her window.

"I'm fine," Laura said. "Just getting excited now that we're actually here. I've only waited fifty-one years for this." She spotted sheep on a hillside. Not that they didn't have sheep in Michigan, but these were *Scottish* sheep, eating *Scottish* grass.

"Same here," Molly said. "I'm so glad you talked us into this, Laura."

"I know Agnes McVie is your hero," Carol said, "but I can't wait to see what she has to teach us. And to learn Scottish baking techniques in an actual Scottish castle? Why, what a braw idea."

The ladies chuckled over Carol's use of a Scottishism commonly heard in Loch Mallaig, a town settled in the early 1800s by Scottish pioneers that retained much of the homeland's customs, colloquialisms, and, in the case of some residents, brogues.

"I've watched Agnes McVie's shows and own all her cookbooks, but I never thought I'd actually meet her." Laura grinned. "And I can't think of anyone I'd rather do it with than my favorite former college roommates and current partners in crime."

Molly tucked a lock of blonde hair behind her ear. "We took a chance closing the bakehouse for ten days so soon after we opened, but I think that the risk will reap rewards when we can advertise the fact that we've trained with Agnes McVie." As the group's PR mastermind, she had a keen sense for marketing. "I'm just grateful that Harvey was willing to watch Angus."

"You may have a hard time getting your Scottie back. Harvey's ego can only take so much of Pascal's indifference." Carol laughed, no doubt picturing her husband cuddling with Molly's beloved Scottish terrier while the MacCallans' cat hid under a bed, as usual. "Speaking of which, have either of you heard from anyone at home?" The ever-organized Carol had overseen the purchase of overseas SIM cards for their cell phones, which they'd swapped in upon landing in Edinburgh.

Laura had never been married and Molly had been widowed for more than ten years, so unlike Carol, they didn't have husbands waiting for them in Loch Mallaig. However, Molly's twenty-seven-year-old daughter, Chloe, and Laura's brother, Brody, had both requested frequent updates about their Highland adventures, so they checked their phones.

"I don't have any texts," Molly said. "Chloe is working double shifts at the veterinary clinic this week, though, so she's pretty much off the grid."

"Nothing from Fergus?" Carol asked innocently.

"No," Molly answered quickly. Laura couldn't see her face, but she was pretty sure her friend's cheeks were bright pink. Fergus MacGregor, who had helped them get their bakery on its feet, had been Molly's teenage crush, and they'd rekindled their friendship—and nothing more, Molly insisted—since the women had moved to Loch Mallaig.

"I don't have any messages either," Laura reported. "But I bet service is spotty out here." They were in the heart of the mountains, quite close to Ben Nevis, the country's highest peak at over 4,000 feet, and her phone didn't display any reception bars.

The road grew steeper and even more narrow, the hills crowding close on each side. Laura thought they should be going down rather than up, since the hotel was on the water, but hesitated to say anything. Former math teacher and current bookkeeping expert Carol had assured them that she'd mapped out the entire trip, door to door.

After a few more minutes of the car grinding uphill, Molly glanced over at Carol. "We're on the right road, correct?"

In response, Carol's shoulders hunched and she gripped the wheel tighter. "There was a choice of two routes and I chose this one. I thought it'd be more scenic."

"It is that," Laura said.

"Chocolate?" Molly pulled out a bar and broke off pieces. "I bought this at the airport."

Laura blessed Molly's wisdom as she took a piece. She bit into it and allowed it to melt on her tongue. It was creamy and rich, and it dissolved some of the tension in the car.

The vehicle finally achieved the crest and began heading downhill. "There's the loch," Carol said, relief evident in her voice. "We're going the right way."

They wound down into the valley, the mist thickening the lower they went. Still visible in the fog were more sheep, an occasional crumbling cottage, stacked stone walls, a man on horseback.

Wait, what? Laura squinted into the mist. It parted slightly, revealing a horse cantering through a field. To Laura's delight, the rider was dressed in a red tartan kilt and plaid, his legs bare save for knee socks, and a tam topped his curly locks. Maybe people up here wore traditional clothing and used horses rather than cars.

"Do you see that?" Molly asked. "He's like something out of the past."

"What are you looking at?" Carol pulled her gaze away from the road for a quick glance. "You're right."

"There are some more people wearing kilts," Laura pointed out. In a grassy hollow, two men circled each other warily, and to her surprise, she saw they were carrying swords. Surely that wasn't how they settled disputes here. A woman with flowing auburn hair stood to one side. Her clothing too was traditional Highlands, with a long plaid draped over her flowing skirt.

Carol slowed the car to a crawl. "What on earth is going on? Should we call 911?"

"Over here it's 999," Laura corrected. She'd picked up that tidbit while standing in line at customs and reading wall signs.

Molly suddenly clapped her hands and issued a squeal of glee. "There's Charlotte Martin!" As the others continued to give her puzzled glances, she added, "The star of *A Highland Lass*? The TV show?" She sighed in exasperation. "Haven't you ever watched it?"

"No," Carol and Laura said in unison.

"It's a story about star-crossed lovers from warring Highland clans set in the mid-1700s," Molly said. "There's lots of real history and the costumes are to die for. And so is the male lead, Finn Paterson."

As Laura continued watching, the man on horseback swept into the clearing, pausing only long enough to sweep Charlotte onto his saddle before spurring his horse on. A chill ran down Laura's spine and she broke out in goose bumps. Even without a soundtrack, the scene was thrilling.

"There he is," Molly said. "Rescuing Ainslee again. That's the name of Charlotte's character."

"Wow. Talk about swoon worthy," said the usually pragmatic Carol. Her bright brown eyes shone with excitement. "How often do you get to see something like that?"

"Or your favorite television show being filmed." Molly's nose was practically pressed to the window glass as they drove by the scene. A short distance on, they saw the film crew, which had previously been hidden behind a cluster of trees. At angry gestures from a couple of people, Carol hit the gas.

Wincing, Laura hoped their car—or its engine noise—hadn't been caught on camera. But they hadn't seen any signs closing the road.

As they drove down the hill, the fog obligingly parted, revealing the shores of Loch Glenellen and a small cluster of houses and other stone buildings beside it. A little way inland from the village, a beautiful manor house stood on a hill. And straight ahead, like something out of a fairy tale, was Glenellen Castle, a sweep of gray stone ornamented with towers, turrets, and battlements. The trio all gasped at the sight.

"It's gorgeous," Laura said. The pictures she'd seen online hadn't done it justice.

As they descended the grade, the castle was lost behind trees. At the bottom of the hill, the road intersected with another. Here, thankfully, was a signpost informing them that the castle could be accessed to the left, along with the village. Glenellen Manor, a stately yet elegant stone house, was to the right.

"The manor looks intriguing too," Molly said. "I wonder if it's open to the public."

"I hope so," Laura said. "I want to see everything I can while we're here." She felt an urgency to savor every second of this experience.

A tall wall soon appeared to their right, a sign they were close to the castle entrance. Then Laura spotted massive iron gates beside a charming stone gatehouse. A plaque attached to the wall announced that this was indeed Glenellen Castle.

The gates were open so Carol drove in, the small sedan's tires crunching on gravel. The curving lane provided sweeping vistas of leafy trees, colorful flower gardens, and lush rolling lawns. Laura had a very real sense of stepping back in time, to a period when they would have approached the castle on horseback or in a carriage.

At last they emerged from a final band of trees and reached the castle's courtyard. The building towered over them as Carol continued along the circular drive to the front entrance, marked by a portico.

"Here we are, ladies." Carol shut off the engine. "After we get checked in, I'll see where they want me to park the car."

After a long drive, they climbed out with stretches and groans. The place was quiet, with the sound of songbirds drifting on the breeze. The air carried fragrances of freshly cut grass and something blooming.

Laura felt all her tensions drop away. In an impulse she gathered the other two women into a group hug. "We're going to have the best time. I just know it."

As the massive wooden front door opened, a huge black dog ran out, panting.

"Minnie, heel," a slender woman with an unlined face and a gray bob called from the doorway. "Don't mind her, lasses. She'll do no harm." The woman's Scottish accent was slight but charming.

Minnie was more interested in slobbering on their shoes than anything else, and she paid her mistress very little mind, if any. Molly smiled and gave the Newfoundland's scruff a vigorous scratch while Carol opened the car's trunk and began depositing bags onto the flagstones.

Laura waved at the silver-haired woman. "We're here for the baking workshop. Are you Lady Freya Cameron?" she asked, having been the one who'd contacted the castle owner to book their stay.

"I am indeed. You must be the three ladies from Michigan. Welcome to Glenellen Castle." Lady Freya stepped out of the portico. "Do you need help with your bags? I can call my husband."

"We packed fairly light, so I think we'll be okay," Carol answered. "But thank you."

"Your car is fine here for now," Lady Freya said. "Let's get you settled." She grabbed a couple of totes, and as a group, they entered the castle, Minnie padding along behind them.

Laura sucked in a breath at the sight of the magnificent entrance hall, with its painted ceiling two stories above, impressive chandeliers, and grand staircase winding up. Carved wood was everywhere—over arched doorways, ornamenting the surround of a massive fireplace, and lining the walls. She also noticed hints of red-and-green fabric here and there, and was surprised at how it added to the elegance of the hall.

"Lady Freya, can you tell us about this fabric?" Molly asked, apparently noticing it as well.

"That's Clan Cameron's traditional tartan," Lady Freya explained, trotting toward a tall reception desk. "We like to show pride in it here." She set the totes down carefully and went behind the counter.

Here, in stark contrast to the tasteful, historic room, stood a sleek computer and printer.

While they waited, Laura glanced around, noting the sheer sense of history in the place. Crossed swords and a couple of shields hung on the wall above the fireplace. Through an archway, she caught glimpses of statues on stands and walls hung with oil paintings. She craned her neck to peek through another open doorway behind the check-in counter—and met the gaze of an older man seated at a desk.

With a jolt at being caught staring, Laura issued a quick smile, then glanced away. Her sights rested on a portrait of a young man hanging on the wall, a cravat around his neck and an aloof expression on his handsome face. A moment later, she felt a presence at her side.

"That is the fifteenth Earl of Glenellen," the older man said in a cultured voice, gesturing toward the painting with the half-glasses he'd just removed. "I am the thirtieth. The first structure on this property was built in the fourteenth century, more of a stronghold than anything. You can see remnants of the castle's history all through the place, if you know where to look."

"Don't let on to Alan if you like history," Freya announced, tapping away at the computer. "He'll talk your ear off." But the smile she sent him was fond.

Lord Alan swung his glasses by the earpiece. "I'm working on a series of biographies about Scottish kings and queens, so I am rather immersed. You must forgive me if I bore you."

Hamish would love to meet Lord Alan, Laura thought. Their part-time bakehouse employee was a retired history teacher and fascinated by Scottish history—he could also be a bit prickly, so she made a mental note to learn everything she could to share with him when they got home, thinking that plying him with factoids might soften his edges a little.

"We're from a town that revels in its Scottish roots," Molly said.

"So believe me, we'd love a tour of the castle and to hear any stories about your ancestors."

Lord Alan beamed. "That's fantastic." He folded the glasses and hung them in the V of his sweater's collar. "I've got a good one for you." He leaned a little closer, dropping his voice to almost a whisper. "They say there's a stash of gold hidden somewhere on this property. Left behind by Bonnie Prince Charlie's men after his failed attempt to regain the throne."

Carol sucked in a breath of excitement. "I know about Bonnie Prince Charlie. His grandfather, King James, was exiled to Europe when William and Mary took the throne. In 1745, Prince Charlie led an uprising based in Scotland."

"That's right," Lord Alan said. "The uprising failed miserably, leading to the dissolution of the clans. Scotland has never been the same." He leaned against the front desk, obviously making himself comfortable for a good, long chat.

"Away with you, my dear." Lady Freya waved at her husband. "You can have this discussion later. I need to get our guests settled." She placed printed pages on the countertop for them to sign.

Her husband took the scolding in good grace, ambling back to his office with a promise to catch up later.

After the ladies signed the registration forms, Lady Freya gave them each a key. "I've put you together in the east wing," she said. "Those rooms have en suite bathrooms and a view of the loch." She circled their rooms on a floor plan of the castle.

"Sounds perfect," Molly enthused. "We're so happy to be here."

"And we're glad to have you with us." Lady Freya handed a printed program to each woman. "This is the schedule for the baking classes. They will begin tomorrow after breakfast. Now let me show you to your rooms."

Laura scrutinized the schedule on the way along the upstairs corridor, which seemed to stretch forever. She smiled as she read over the topics: Scotch pies, almond lace cookies, oatcakes, sticky toffee pudding. All familiar dishes, but she was eager to find out what Agnes McVie could teach them about each one.

Molly, on the other hand, had her mind on different matters. "We noticed them filming *A Highland Lass* on the way here," she said to their hostess. "I'm a big fan."

"Some of the cast and crew are staying here, in the west wing." Lady Freya sent Molly a smile. "Including Charlotte Martin."

Molly practically swooned. "You mean I might get to meet her?"

"I expect so," her ladyship said. "She'll be here at least until the end of this week." She stopped in front of a door. "This is you, Carol." Using her master key, she unlocked the door and stood back to let Carol enter.

Laura followed along inside. The room wasn't huge, but it was furnished with a canopy bed and carved antique furniture. Thick carpets and wall hangings gave it a cozy feel. Freya showed Carol the bathroom—once a dressing room—and Carol set down her bags. "I want to see your rooms," she said to Laura and Molly.

Molly's room was similar, but with a blue theme instead of red. Laura's was decorated in pale yellow, and she couldn't wait to take a long bath in the slipper tub and maybe even pretend she was a member of the royal family.

"You must be exhausted from your travels," Lady Freya said. "If you want, I can bring up a tray. I recommend you get a good night's sleep."

The trio accepted their hostess's offer with gratitude. Laura knew she wasn't up to eating in public right now. The friends decided to unpack and rest, then gather to eat when the food arrived in an hour or so.

After the others had left, Laura hung her clothing in the closet and put her toiletry bag in the bathroom. Then she opened the curtains wide to the view of the loch and plopped on the bed to rest for a bit.

Her break didn't last long. Excitement overcame her physical exhaustion, and she sprang to her feet. She wasn't going to waste a minute of this precious trip. She made a circuit of the room, studying the handwoven tapestries and ornately framed oil paintings. There was carved wainscoting and one wall was fully paneled. She ran her hand along the satiny wood, admiring the carved thistles and other emblems. No one did work like this anymore. Who could afford it?

Something clicked under her touch. Not sure if she'd imagined the sound, Laura pressed on the panel again. A length of wood separated from the one beside it. Laura's heart began to pound. Was this a secret doorway? She'd heard of such things and had always wanted to see one in real life.

She slid her fingernails between the panels and tugged gently, and the opening widened enough for her to peer inside. Cool air brushed past her face, which meant there was ventilation somewhere. Laura stepped inside the opening. The shaft of light from her room revealed that she was on a landing, with shadowy stairs going up and down. She had found a secret staircase.

Carol and Molly have to see this. She turned to go back out, but to her shock, the opening slid shut without a sound.

Laura was trapped in the dark.

2

For a long moment, Laura stood in the dusty dark, not quite sure what had just happened. Then she barked a laugh. "Well, that'll teach me," she murmured as she returned to the wall and used her fingers to try and find the opening.

But there was nothing. The wall had sealed so seamlessly that she couldn't even feel where the doorway had been.

Time for plan B. Laura pounded on the wall with both fists. "Anybody there? Help! I'm trapped!"

No one came. Laura leaned against the wall. Was she going to be stuck here forever? She grimaced as images of skeletons from other unfortunates flashed into her mind. Then she rolled her eyes. *Carol and Molly will realize you're missing and look for you.* But had she locked her door? Her brave attitude nearly cracked at the question. No, she'd left it open, she was pretty sure.

Trying to ignore the fears circling her head like bats—and she certainly hoped there weren't any of those in here!—Laura slid down to the floor and sat with her back against the wall. She had to be patient and wait, that was all. She'd certainly learned her lesson. No exploring secret passageways, at least not without a light. Even her cell phone would help, but that was sitting on the bedside table.

How much longer was she going to be in here? Their meals should be arriving soon. She'd spent at least half an hour unpacking and examining her room.

At a muffled noise, Laura leaped to her feet, her ear pressed to the wall. Was that a voice? Straining to listen, she definitely heard voices getting louder and rising in inquiry. Then she distinctly heard Carol call, "Laura? Where did you go?"

She banged on the wall. "I'm in here!" she yelled. "Behind the wall." When there was no response, she pounded harder, with every ounce of strength she had.

"Laura? Are you in there?" Carol called.

Someone knocked on the wall and Laura rapped back eagerly.

"Hang on," Molly called. "We're going to get you out."

Laura waited, her heart thumping in her chest. She liked adventure as much as anyone, but suddenly she couldn't wait to get out, to see sunlight and breath fresh air, to see the faces of her—

Click. The panel slid open. "There you are, my girl." Lady Freya gestured. "Why don't you step out of there?"

"I thought you'd never ask," Laura said, slipping through the gap. Both of her friends were hovering nearby, anxiety etching their faces. They gathered Laura into a group hug.

Lady Freya closed the panel. "I'm going to have to put up a warning sign, I suppose. Or block the opening with furniture." She swung around to wag a finger at Laura. "We can't have guests disappearing on us."

"I appreciate the rescue," Laura said, brushing dust and cobwebs off her sweater. "I opened the passageway by accident and then I couldn't resist going inside. I had no idea it would close on me."

"There's a latch on the other side," Lady Freya said. "You must have hit it."

"Is it a secret room or a secret passage?" Carol asked, running her hand along the paneling.

"There's a staircase that goes down to the kitchen as well as up to the tower," Lady Freya answered.

"Ah, so it's just servant access," Carol said.

Lady Freya held up a finger. "Not entirely. It was built in the days when people—like priests—had to hide."

"Including Bonnie Prince Charlie?" Molly asked, her eyes glowing with interest. "Do you think gold is hidden in the castle, like your husband said?"

The lady scoffed. "No, that's only a myth. If all the gold Charlie was supposed to have hidden was found, you could pave the streets of Edinburgh."

Laura nodded. Like many tall tales, the rumor of gold was probably for entertainment purposes only. Besides, if there actually was a hidden treasure, surely it would have been found by now, over two hundred years after Charlie had fled Scotland.

Apparently tired of the topic, her ladyship said, "If there's anything else you need, give me a ring on the house phone. Otherwise, enjoy your evening." She bustled toward Laura's door, which stood open to the hall.

"Our food is in my room," Carol said. "I have a big table so we can eat in there."

"She brought us chicken stew and bannock bread," Molly said. "I can't wait to try it."

At the mention of the tasty biscuit-like bread baked in a cast iron skillet, Laura's stomach rumbled. "Let's go. I'm starving."

Laura's first night in a Scottish castle passed peacefully and she woke up refreshed. She opened the curtains to a view of sunlight sparkling on the loch and not a speck of fog anywhere. From here, she could see the hills surrounding the water like a bowl, a touch of white on the peaks where snow still lingered.

Stunning. Absolutely stunning. Laura inhaled a deep breath of gratitude at this opportunity to experience life in Scotland, however brief. Someone knocked at her door. "Come in," she called.

Carol popped her head in. "We're going down to breakfast in ten. Will you be ready?"

"Sure. Let me get dressed and I'll be over." Laura had taken a bath to rid herself of any remaining cobwebs after her secret passage adventure, so all she needed to do was brush her teeth and run a comb through her shoulder-length auburn hair.

Laura put on a fresh pair of jeans and a quirky T-shirt from a food festival she'd attended in upstate New York a few years earlier, then slipped her feet into some low-heeled boots, assuming they'd be standing at cooking stations for the workshop.

Not that she was a stranger to long hours on her feet—as the former head chef at trendy Manhattan restaurant 29 North, she felt as though she'd spent more hours standing than sitting for the past few decades. She'd thrived on the late nights and high-pressure atmosphere of the New York City restaurant scene. But after a visit to her aging parents in Michigan the previous summer, she'd found herself longing to be closer to them, as well as Brody and his family. When she'd confessed that to Carol and Molly on a girlfriends' trip the next month, they'd also admitted to craving a midlife change. Less than a year later, the three women—whom Fergus had dubbed the Bakehouse Three—had cut the ribbon at Bread on Arrival's grand opening.

Laura stood and bounced a little in her boots, deciding that they'd be perfect for a morning of cooking lessons, and even for a walk in the afternoon if they had time. In the room's local guide, it said the village was less than a mile away following a path along the loch.

She popped her billfold into her tote to take downstairs, not willing to let her passport or wallet out of her sight. She was just locking her door behind her when Carol and Molly emerged from their rooms.

"Good morning," Laura greeted her friends.

"*Guid mornin*," Carol answered with a sparkle in her eyes. She seemed to remember a new phrase used by her father's Scottish parents every day.

"Let's get some breakfast." Laura grinned. "Or is there something else I should be calling it?"

"Breakfast works fine for me," Carol said.

Molly studied a tourist map of the area as they descended the stairs. "I want to go shopping later. We need souvenirs."

"I have to bring the kids something." Carol laughed. "Including Harvey." Carol's daughter, Jenny and her husband, Craig, had school-age twins, Maisie and Gavin. They lived in Loch Mallaig and were a large part of the reason Carol and Harvey had relocated from Pittsburgh.

"The fun part is deciding what to buy," Laura said. "I like to find locally made crafts whenever I travel."

"That will be our mission," Molly said. "And yes, I accept it." She pulled her gaze from her map to point out a corridor opening off the lobby. "The dining room is that way."

The dining room was spacious, with green-and-cream embossed wallpaper and several round tables dotting the floral-patterned carpet. On one side, a pleasant fire crackled under a carved mantel, and on the other stood a long table holding urns and chafing dishes. Lady Freya stood at the table, checking something under a lid.

"Good morning, ladies," she said. "I trust you slept well?"

The women all assented.

"Glad to hear it." Lady Freya gestured to the buffet. "We've got tea, coffee, and juice. To eat, there's oatmeal as well as a full Scottish breakfast." She pointed to a smaller table. "Over there we have fruit, yogurt, and cold cereal for lighter appetites."

"I want the full breakfast," Molly said. "When in Rome, right?" She set down her bag at one of the tables and the others did the same. Then they lined up at the buffet, filling gilt-edged china plates and cups.

"Did you make all of this yourself?" Laura asked Lady Freya, thinking that their hostess would need professional training to handle all the cooking alone. The full breakfast included beans, eggs, fried mushrooms and tomatoes, an assortment of breakfast meats, and golden tattie scones made from potatoes—and it smelled amazing.

Lady Freya laughed. "Certainly not. We have a cook, Mrs. Beasley. She does most meals, though we use caterers for events. Here she comes now." A tall and very thin woman with iron-gray waves and a forbidding expression swept into the dining room carrying a serving pan.

"Everything looks wonderful," Laura said to Mrs. Beasley, who merely glanced down her nose with a sniff as she replenished the black pudding and bacon. Laura took some of each, not scared off by black pudding's real name, blood sausage. After adding a scoop of mixed berries to her plate, she joined the others at their table.

"Yum," Carol said, pushing a piece of tattie scone through egg yolk. "This is delicious. Everything tastes so fresh."

Laura pulled out her phone and took a picture of her full plate. "This is what I call culinary research." She cut a piece of black pudding and popped it into her mouth, chewing with appreciation at the mix of flavors.

"You'll have to share that photo with me for our social media page," Molly said.

"Sure," Laura agreed. "Though maybe don't identify the blood sausage by name."

"Good advice." Molly winked, then tucked in to her own helpings of oatmeal, bacon, and fruit.

They were about halfway through the meal when two men and two women came in together. Recognizing one of the women—who could forget that glorious head of red hair, even if it was tightly restrained in a bun this morning?—Laura whispered to Molly, "Isn't that Charlotte?"

Molly glanced over, her eyes widening, and nodded. Then noticing where Laura's attention had refocused, she added, "And that's Finn."

Although she'd met her share of celebrity diners at 29 North, Laura couldn't help but stare at the handsome young actor. Despite being casually dressed in jeans and a fleece pullover, Finn had undeniable magnetism. His chiseled face and dark curls were perfect for his role as a Scottish hero.

The other man was shorter and slighter, with a balding head and wire-rimmed glasses. But what he lacked in good looks, he made up for in attitude. His sharp eyes went everywhere, landing on Laura with a glare. When she frowned in response, he broke eye contact and got in line for food. As the line edged forward, he talked to the second woman, who had a slim build and thick coppery hair pulled back in a ponytail.

"The man in glasses is Clive O'Connor, the director," Molly murmured to Carol and Laura. "I've seen him in photos at parties with the cast." She tipped her chin toward the copper-haired woman. "And that's Kyla Paterson, Finn's sister. She's also in the show."

Now that Laura had that information, she could see a family resemblance. Besides similar eyes, Kyla had a dimpled chin like Finn, but hers was much more feminine. She was pretty, if not eye-catching and charismatic like Charlotte. *Star power is an elusive thing.* Perfect features didn't guarantee it, she realized. It was something innate.

Over by the coffee urn, Finn touched Charlotte on the shoulder and leaned close. She shrugged him off with a glare.

"Quit it," Charlotte hissed, loud enough that the women heard.

Finn stared down at the star, his face forlorn, but she ignored him as she finished filling her cup and marched off. She sat down at a table near the American women, then sipped at her coffee, staring into the distance with a moody expression.

Clive and Kyla joined Charlotte. "Aren't you eating?" Kyla asked, a spiteful edge to her tone. She picked up a piece of toast and bit into it, her eyes on Charlotte's face.

"I will in a minute," Charlotte said. "I can't eat a thing until I have my first cup of coffee."

"Is she French?" Laura whispered to Molly. "She has a slight accent."

"Raised there," Molly said. "But on screen, her accent is pure Scots."

Finn came to the table with a loaded plate, careful to sit across from Charlotte, not next to her despite the empty chairs. "Any news from the network about next season?" he asked Clive, pulling up to the table.

Clive, head down over his plate while he ate, gave a surly shrug. "You'll be the first to know. Right now the important thing is to make this season irresistible."

Kyla fixed her gaze on the director. "So we're not looking to make any casting changes." She cut her eyes toward Charlotte when she said this, who jumped, then set her cup carefully on the table. What was that about?

The director growled. "Certainly not until I hear back from the network. We've finally achieved the right mix, and we'd better keep it if we have any hope of a third season."

"I sure hope we get renewed," Finn said, his voice deep and resonant. "We're finally building momentum with fans."

"You are, anyway," Kyla said. "Remember those rowdy women in Edinburgh? And the one who sneaked onto a closed set?"

Finn groaned. "How could I forget? She surprised me on the way to my dressing room and asked me to marry her."

"Ridiculous." Clive shook his head. "Hopefully we're far enough out in the countryside to prevent a repeat of that incident."

Charlotte, who had seemed lost in her own thoughts, pushed back from the table. "I guess I will get something to eat." Her voice sounded brittle, and Finn stared after her in concern. She dithered at the food table, then returned a few minutes later with a small bowl of oatmeal and a side plate of sausages.

Laura returned her attention to her friends, and they all exchanged guilty looks for having caught each other eavesdropping.

"Does anyone have the class schedule handy?" Molly asked, refocusing them on the day ahead.

"I do," Carol said, reaching into her bag. She was seated between the other two so they read over her shoulder. "The first lesson starts with piecrust."

"Oh no." Molly groaned. "I have never been able to make piecrust. It's either too wet or too dry, and I usually have to patch the crust into a pan like a jigsaw puzzle."

Laura gave her friend a comforting smile. "You have to find the techniques that work for you. I've failed enough to know that for certain."

"Really?" Molly asked, her voice skeptical. "Everything you make is perfect."

"That's because I hide my mistakes in the trash." Laura winked, then picked up her cup. "And I'm sure Agnes McVie has as much to teach me as either of you."

After finishing their coffee and breakfast, the trio had a little while before class started, so they explored the ground floor of the castle. They found a charming sitting room overlooking the loch, a billiards room complete with taxidermy trophies, and a two-story library featuring a rolling set of steps that reached the upper shelves. Once one of the thousands of volumes had been chosen, comfortable leather chairs and sofas offered the perfect spot to curl up and read.

"I could stay in here and read forever," Molly said in wonder.

"I'm glad you like my humble abode." With a chuckle at this understatement, Lord Alan stepped further into the library from the opposite end. He carried a laptop case under his arm.

"Where did you come from?" Laura asked, not seeing another entrance besides the one she and her friends had used.

"There's a hidden doorway in the paneling," Lord Alan said. "The castle is absolutely rife with architectural eccentricities." He moved to a long table, where he set down his computer.

Laura laughed. "Don't I know it. I discovered one in my room."

"You must be in the Primrose Room," the laird said, apparently referencing the yellow wallpaper. He opened his laptop and pressed a few keys. "I'll be happy to talk to you about the history of this place, if you're interested."

"I am," Molly said, and the others assented. "But right now, we need to get to our baking lesson. Could you tell us how to get to the kitchen?"

On the way down the corridor after receiving Lord Alan's instructions, Carol held up her map of the castle. "We could have used this, you know."

"True," Molly agreed, "but I love listening to the laird speak. It's like living in an episode of *A Highland Lass*."

"It's so fun to be immersed in Scottish life," Laura said. "I keep thinking about Hamish and how much he'd love to be here."

"Yes, he probably has an ancestor from Glenellen too," Molly said with a chuckle. Hamish somehow managed to work his purported familial ties to former king of Scotland Robert the Bruce into many a conversation.

After a few more zigzags through the corridors, they reached the enormous kitchen, which featured a flagstone floor and brick arches defining different work areas. Although one wall was lined with ancient cast iron ovens and a hearth large enough to roast an ox, the other equipment was state-of-the-art.

"Oh," Laura said, stopping short in the doorway. "I'm suffering from a severe case of kitchen envy."

"Me too," Molly admitted. "And I'm a novice compared to you."

As they strolled further into the space, they spotted a plump woman with an auburn bun hunched over a long wooden table. She wore a khaki dress covered with a bib apron and was writing intently in a notebook.

Laura elbowed her friends and murmured, "That's Agnes McVie, our instructor." She felt her face flush with excitement. "One of the most famous pastry chefs in the world."

As the trio drew closer, Carol cleared her throat as a warning so as not to startle the distracted woman. Agnes stood upright and turned, her small, pale eyes taking in every detail of the three women. In response, Laura stood up straighter, suddenly wishing she'd chosen to wear something more professional than an old T-shirt.

"You must be my students," Agnes said in a clipped tone as she scrutinized them with a frown. "At least you're on time. Lessons will begin and end at the appointed hour. We have much to do."

Laura glanced at Molly, whose eyes were glassy with what looked like fear. As the least experienced baker, she was likely nervous to work with someone like Agnes. "If you can handle Hamish, you can handle her," Laura muttered to Molly, who laughed and relaxed a little.

The Bakehouse Three introduced themselves, and Agnes's frown softened into a curious expression. "Laura Donovan, you say?" she repeated as though trying to place the name.

"I used to be the chef at 29 North," Laura supplied.

"Ah, that's it." Agnes paused. "Your beef Wellington was quite satisfactory."

Swelling with pride at what was likely a high compliment, Laura beamed. "Thank you."

"Why ever did you leave?" Agnes asked. "Wasn't Jacques paying you enough?"

In fact, Laura's old boss, restaurateur Jacques Bileaux, had offered her quite a hefty raise if she'd reconsider and stay on. "It was time for a new adventure," she told Agnes, then gestured toward Carol and Molly. "We've opened a Scottish bakehouse together, and we're here to learn from the best."

Before Agnes could respond to the flattery, Lady Freya hurried into the kitchen, her soft leather shoes almost noiseless on the flagstones. "Oh good, you're here," she said when she drew close to Carol and Molly.

Agnes put a hand on Laura's arm. "Excuse me." She turned to Lady Freya. "I presume the other students are on their way?"

"Oh, I . . . well, they . . ." Lady Freya wrung her hands in dismay. Finally she swallowed hard and said, "They called this morning. They're all quite ill."

The instructor rested her fists on her substantial hips. "That won't do, Lady Freya. I must have six students at the very least. If not, the class is canceled."

Laura exchanged glances with her friends. Had they crossed an ocean for nothing?

3

Laura, Carol, and Molly wore matching frowns, each of them clearly thinking the same thing: *What a disaster*. If the baking class was canceled, not only was the trip a waste of time and money on their part, it would also be a severe disappointment.

Lady Freya was equally taken aback. "Agnes, let's not discuss this here." As she ushered the instructor away, she said over her shoulder, "Please feel free to help yourself to a snack. We'll be in my office." On a counter to one side stood pitchers of ice water, a bowl of fruit, and a tray of cookies.

Laura sank against the counter with a groan. "I can't believe this."

"I guess we bought ourselves an expensive vacation." Carol folded her arms. "It's not like we can write it off as a business expense now."

"I don't understand why the number of students matters," Molly said. "The class fees are nonrefundable, so it's not as if Agnes isn't going to get paid."

Laura lowered her voice. "If she's like other celebrity chefs I've known, it's about ego. She doesn't want word to get out that her class bombed."

"What if we found some more students?" Molly suggested. "I'll bet people in the village would love to join in."

The three women stopped talking as Charlotte Martin walked into the kitchen and glanced around. "Have you seen Lady Freya?" the actress asked.

"She's meeting with someone in her office," Laura answered. "Can we give her a message?"

Charlotte thought for a second. "All right. We have the morning off while some village scenes are being shot, so I wanted to talk to her about lunch."

"Do you feel like taking a baking lesson with Agnes McVie?" Molly blurted, her cheeks pinking. "It's going to be fun."

The actress's eyes widened. "Are you serious?" At first, Laura worried Charlotte was about to say something cruel, but then she beamed and nodded. "Yes, I think I would. I love to bake."

"Fantastic." Laura grinned at her friend's creative solution—but the problem wasn't completely solved yet. "Now we need two more people. Any ideas?"

Charlotte thought for a moment then smiled. "Actually, yes. I'll be right back."

Carol pushed up her sleeves. "And I'm going to tell Lady Freya that the day is saved."

A short while later, the six students, each wearing a white baker's apron, stood behind one of the long tables while Agnes began the lesson. She'd been extremely pleased to have Charlotte, Kyla, and Finn in the class and had insisted on photographs being taken of herself with the actors. Finn especially looked handsome in his apron.

"Today we are learning to make individual Scotch pies, starting with the crust," Agnes said. "It's a simple process, but one that trips up a lot of people."

Molly raised her hand slightly. "Like me."

Agnes acknowledged her comment with a nod. "This is a hot water crust, with only four ingredients."

The chef had her students chop up chunks of white, creamy lard, then measure and add to the water with a small amount of salt. Once the water was boiling, it was added to bowls of flour and quickly stirred, then kneaded.

"This is easy," Charlotte said as she worked the warm, soft dough with her fingers.

"Reminds me of being a kid," Finn said. He worked intently, tongue between his teeth.

Kyla, standing between Charlotte and Finn, laughed. "I remember making biscuits and you putting dough in my hair." She shook her curls. "Took forever to clean out." Finn feinted attacking his sister with dough, and she ducked with a squeal.

"No food fights in my kitchen," Agnes said, keeping a stern eye on the playful pair until they subsided with snickers. Hands behind her back, she strolled back and forth watching the cooks. "Once the dough is smooth, break off about a quarter and wrap it in plastic. That will be the lid for your pie." She instructed them to set their dough aside for ten minutes so it could cool, then demonstrated how to wind plastic wrap around a small jam jar. "This will be used to shape the dough."

"I'd use deep muffin pans in the shop," Laura told Carol and Molly, knowing this method would be slow going in a bakery. "That way, I can make dozens at a time."

After the dough cooled enough, they pressed out circles and shaped it up around the jars, trying to get it even. Then the jars went into the refrigerator.

"While those are setting up, we'll work on the mince filling," Agnes said. She retrieved a bowl of ground lamb from the walk-in cooler. "If the class were longer, I'd have you grind your own filling, but it is what it is."

At Agnes's instruction, each student added spices, salt and pepper, and a little stock to their filling and stirred it thoroughly.

"This is fun," Carol said. "I can't wait to taste it."

Molly nodded. "Exactly what I was thinking."

They set their bowls of filling aside and retrieved their dough, still wrapped around the jars.

"I'm going to teach you a trick," Agnes said. "How do you suppose we are going to get the crust away from the jars?"

"Scrape down around it with a knife?" Finn suggested.

"That won't work," Laura said, recalling many a ruined pie shell. "Ask me how I know." As she laughed, the young star gave her a warm smile. *If only I were twenty years younger . . . and he didn't clearly have eyes only for Charlotte.*

Agnes picked up a steaming kettle from the stove. "It's very simple. We're going to add hot—not boiling—water to each jar." She went around and poured, careful not to splash. She set the kettle down again. "Now, hold the pastry gently with one hand and twist the jar up and out with the other."

"It worked!" Molly exclaimed in triumph, holding up a perfect deep, round shell ready to fill and bake.

Laura smiled at her friend's enthusiasm, glad that the amateur baker's first project was a success. As she filled her own Scotch pie, shaped her remaining pastry for a lid, and crimped the top in a fluted design, her spirits soared. Despite a rocky start, this workshop was going to be one of the most memorable experiences of their lives. She could feel it.

"Where to first?" Carol asked. After sampling their Scotch pies for lunch, the Bakehouse Three had set out on a nice, long walk on the Glenellen Castle grounds.

Laura gazed at the loch glinting in the sunshine, drawn to the water as though it were magnetized. "We could explore the gardens here first, then maybe wander down to the village."

Molly consulted her map, which was already worn on the folds and stained with a coffee cup ring. "Definitely doable to walk to the village and back." She pointed out the route on the map. "See where the path begins at the edge of the castle property?"

Carol made a sweeping gesture. "After you, Molly. We'll follow your lead."

Molly tucked the folded map into her bag. "Let's go this way." She led them down a paved path to an opening in a tall hedge.

Laura strolled slowly, identifying the flowers in bloom. Clumps of peonies waved near a small orchard of apple trees covered in pink-and-white blossoms. Petals drifted down from the trees on a light breeze, intensifying the rich floral scents in the air. Bees buzzed and birds sang sweetly, as if personally welcoming them to Scotland.

Beyond the hedge lay a garden of shaped topiaries with a fountain in the middle. A spry elderly man dressed in tweed pants and a thick sweater wielded large clippers, shaping a bush into a more perfect globe. He wore a flat cap, and a wild ginger-and-white beard stood out around his face like a lion's ruff. Wound several times around his neck was a scarf bearing the Cameron clan's traditional red-and-green tartan.

"I've never seen anything like this," Molly said as all three women pulled out their phones, eager to take photographs of the unusual garden.

The gardener spotted them and waved his clippers.

"Oh, I'm sorry," Laura said. "Are we allowed to take pictures?"

The man chuckled. "Please do. Takes me a fair amount of work to keep these in good trim."

"I'll bet." Carol moved closer. "Hi, I'm Carol. My friends and I are staying here for the cooking classes with Agnes McVie."

"Och aye. She's a guid cook, or so I've heard. On the television, even." He clipped a few twigs. "I'm Terry, by the way. I take care of the grounds."

The other two introduced themselves, then Molly said, "How do we get to the footpath to the village? I have a map, but I want to double-check."

"There are many ways," Terry said. "I'll tell you the best two. The shortest path cuts through the woods to the loch." He pointed to an opening in the hedge to their left. "The other is longer but more interesting, since it takes you through the walled gardens. Which do ye prefer?"

"Walled gardens," they answered in unison.

Terry pointed straight. "Off ye go then. But be careful once you're on the loch path. The footing can be tricky, especially near the cliffs in bad weather." He turned back to the bush and resumed clipping.

"Do you think we should still go?" Carol asked when they were out of earshot. "I don't like the sound of tricky footing."

"He said in bad weather." Laura pointed up at the cloudless sky. "Today is perfect. Clear and dry."

"I say we do it," Molly said. "We can always turn around if we change our minds." She marched through the opening in the hedge.

The first walled enclosure was full of low hedges in a geometric pattern. Spicy scents filled the air.

"This is a knot garden," Molly said. "A medieval herb garden."

"Fascinating." Laura bent to study the fragrant plants, breaking off leaves and sniffing their aroma. "Basil, oregano, sage, rosemary. A cook's garden."

Next was a rose garden, many bushes already in bloom—pink, white, yellow, and red. If they hadn't planned to go to the village, Laura would have been happy to laze for hours under the arbor. What an enchanting spot.

The final enclosure was a rock garden built on natural ledges and featuring a mix of thistles, lavender, and native heaths and heathers in various colors.

"This is really different," Carol said. She posed beside a huge thistle plant, careful not to stand too close to the spines. "Can you take a picture of me for Harvey? He'll get a kick out of this plant."

"Of course," Laura said. She took Carol's phone and snapped several. She had the feeling she would have hundreds of pictures of this trip by the time she was done. Around every corner was a photo op.

They emerged from the garden into a grassy field sloping to the water. From here, they could look back and see the castle, set slightly higher on a rise. The glistening loch, framed by sloping hills, was equally stunning.

"Is this real?" Molly asked, echoing Laura's thoughts.

"Standing right here, it could be three hundred years ago," Carol said. "That's what I love about historical places like this."

They found the footpath easily. It was a beaten track through the grass, bordered at times with sprawling shrubs covered in yellow flowers.

"Those are gorse," Laura said, inhaling the coconut scent she'd read about. "It smells good, but they have thorns."

"Pretty at a distance," Carol said, "like some people." That wry comment drew laughs from the other two.

As Terry had mentioned, the path took them onto a rocky headland that tumbled down to a shingled beach below. A steep, narrow track led to the water. They paused once again to take in the view.

"I can see how someone might have an accident in the fog," Carol said, examining the abrupt drop. "There isn't any guardrail."

"That would ruin the ambiance," Molly joked.

Laura could also see herself spending much time here, sitting in the sun on the headland or down on the beach exploring. But at this rate, they'd never make it to the village. "We'd better get moving," she said. "We want to get back to the castle in time for dinner."

"Lead on," Carol said, nudging Molly, and they set off again.

The path led them through a band of woods and out onto another, less precipitous headland where the elegant Glenellen Manor stood in a place of prominence. They could also see the gleaming white houses of the village nestled around a natural cove a short distance ahead.

"I wonder if the manor is open for tours," Laura said. "It's such a beautiful building."

Molly checked her map, which showed places of interest for tourists. "No, it says it's privately owned and not to trespass."

"Maybe there are different rules for stars." Eyebrow raised, Carol pointed. "Look."

Laura followed Carol's finger, and as they watched, Charlotte strolled along a garden path, staring up at the house. Then she squared her shoulders and marched up to the front door, where she rang the bell.

The door opened, revealing a tall, older man dressed in a tweed suit. After speaking to Charlotte briefly, he stood back to let her inside, then shut the door with a solid click the Bakehouse Three could hear from several yards away.

Laura furrowed her brow. *What's that about?*

4

"I guess I was right," Carol said with a laugh, then sighed. "We should take a break soon."

"Agreed." Laura had awakened feeling energized, but her jet lag was catching up to her. "Let's find a tea shop and sit for a while."

"I know just the place." Molly waved the map. "The Library Tearoom."

The path soon intersected with a narrow lane leading between two rows of charming cottages. A little closer to the harbor, they came upon a cluster of buildings that made up the village's business district. There was a pub or two, a post office, several stores, a church, and the promised tea shop at the end. The store windows were filled with enticing goods—tartans, tea cozies, and hand-knit sweaters. They strolled slowly down the lane, previewing items for later shopping.

"Wouldn't Harvey look good in that tam?" Carol asked, nodding toward a flat, plaid cap with a sizable red pom-pom on top.

Actually, Laura could imagine Carol's dashing husband wearing it. "I think he would."

"I'll be back," Carol promised the hat.

"And so will I." Molly sighed over a gorgeous cream fisherman knit sweater in the next window.

The Library Tearoom was right on the harbor, a small whitewashed building with red roses climbing over an arbor that led into a small courtyard bordered by a wrought iron fence. In the courtyard, tables were set on a brick patio featuring strings of lights and potted plants.

"I love it already," Laura said as they approached the shiny black front door. She stepped inside behind Carol, but Molly lingered outside for a moment, likely using her marketing eye to glean inspiration for their bakery.

The tearoom was basically one large room, with a pass-through and swinging door marking the kitchen area behind. The groups of small tables and chairs, the long bakery case and gleaming silver urns, the clatter of dishes and aroma of baked goods felt like home to Laura. But this tearoom had something extra: an area holding several tall bookcases and glass-fronted exhibits. In addition, dozens of old photographs were hung on the walls, local scenes from what Laura could tell.

"Apparently this isn't just a tearoom—it's also a museum and a bookshop," Laura said to her friends as Molly caught up.

"Correction." An elderly woman seated at a table nearby set her teacup down with a clink. Her abundant white hair was piled atop her head, and she wore a plaid shawl over a high-necked blouse. "This is a lending library, not a bookshop. You are welcome to borrow any books you wish."

"That's so nice," Carol said. "We're staying at the castle, but I'll come see you if I don't find anything in their library to pique my interest."

The woman's thin brows rose. "At the castle, are you? That's a rare treat."

"It is," Laura agreed. "But so is this. What a charming shop. And something smells absolutely scrumptious in here."

The woman gave a tinkling laugh. "That would be the scones my granddaughter is baking." She stood. "Let me show you to a table."

She settled them in a corner nook overlooking the garden. "I'm Una, by the way, the proprietor." She handed them small menus with beverages on one side and food on the other.

Molly took the lead with introductions. "The three of us own a bakehouse in Loch Mallaig, Michigan. We're in Scotland seeking inspiration and knowledge to improve our business."

"Och, I've heard of that little slice of the old country in the new." Beaming, Una clasped her hands together. "You must have our sampler then. Small portions of our favorite baked goodies."

"That sounds perfect," Laura said, speaking for the group. She wasn't really hungry after eating her Scotch pie for lunch, and she assumed her friends weren't either . . . but she always had room for dessert.

"Sampler for three with Scottish blend tea?" At their agreement, Una bustled away.

While they waited, Laura studied the photographs on the nearby wall. One in particular caught her eye, and when Una returned with a large tray, she asked, "Is that a picture of a local business?" The building looked like the others in the village, but the sign above the window read, *Mario Rico, Confectioner*. A dark-haired man wearing an apron stood proudly in front, his plump wife beside him.

After passing around teacups and placing a tiered plate full of treats on the table, Una peered at the photo. "It is. Scotland had several waves of Italian immigrants, which many people don't know. They brought us fantastic ice cream, for one thing." Her pleasant features twisted in a grimace. "But during World War II, many Italians were interned for the duration." She smoothed her apron. "A sad episode."

Laura knew a little about internment in the United States, where citizens of certain nationalities had been rounded up and confined as potential spies. She hadn't known that it had happened in Scotland too.

Seemingly eager to change the subject, Una asked, "Did the lady from the castle get the information she was looking for about her family?"

"Which one?" Carol said. "There are several women staying there right now."

"She had red hair." Una shrugged, then glanced around the table. "Are you all set? Please let me know if you need anything." She returned to her seat and resumed knitting away on what looked like a shawl.

"That description didn't narrow it down much," Molly said. "Charlotte, Kyla, and Agnes all have red hair, and there could be redheaded guests we haven't met yet." She selected a tiny slice of pie, reading the printed card aloud. "Ecclefechan Butter Tart. I wonder what this tastes like."

"I don't know, but from the looks of it 'heaven' is probably accurate." Laura read another card aloud. "Selkirk bannock. That's my first pick."

"And I'm having a classic," Carol said. "A scone with clotted cream and jam."

A short while later, Laura pushed away her plate with a groan. "I am literally going to burst."

"Me too," Molly said. "But we had to try everything, right?" She used her fingers to pick up the last few crumbs of oatcake.

Una came to their table to present the check. "Did you find the inspiration you were seeking?" she asked with a smile.

"We sure did," Carol said. "Our customers are going to love us."

"That's the aim, right?" Una's eyes twinkled merrily. "If you want, I can write up some recipe cards for you. It will be a pleasure thinking of our treats being served across the sea."

Laura's brows rose. "Would you really do that?" She stood and gave the elderly tearoom owner an impulsive hug. Una reminded Laura of her late grandmother, whose personal cookbook was a cherished centerpiece of Laura's collection. "Thank you so much."

Una's cheeks reddened and she flapped a hand. "Away wit ye. You're making me blush."

The women paid for the tea and left with promises to return. "Are you still up for some shopping?" Carol asked, her eyes hopeful.

Laura really wanted to stumble back to her room and take a nap, but she didn't want to disappoint her friends. "Of course. Maybe only a couple of stores, though? We can come back another time."

"That's fine," Carol said with relief. "Unlikely as it may be, I'm just worried someone might snatch up that hat."

"Better safe than sorry," Laura said, then followed Carol into the tartan shop. She had a small list to fill too—gifts for her parents, Brody and his wife, Eliza, and their teenagers, Adina and Henry. The three had also agreed they needed to bring back souvenirs for Hamish and his wife, Joyce, as well as their other part-time employee, Bridget.

Carol went right to the counter to buy the hat while Laura and Molly browsed. "Do you think Chloe will like this?" Molly held up a tartan messenger bag. "I can picture her using it to carry charts and files around."

"It's perfect." Laura flipped through a rack of accessories. She held up a pair of tartan earmuffs. "Think Adina will like these?"

Molly nodded. "I bet she would."

"Let's get Bridget a pair too," Laura suggested, thinking that they suited the college student's quirky sense of style.

They continued shopping for a few more minutes, then made their purchases. Next was the woolen shop, where Molly bought her sweater and Carol and Laura found lovely knitted scarves for people on their lists. The local cream-colored wool was gorgeous made up in cable and honeycomb designs.

"Maybe we should have brought the rental car," Carol said as they trudged up the hill out of the village, laden with bags.

"We can on the next trip." Laura focused on planting her feet, step by step. She would sleep well tonight. "But I really enjoyed walking down here."

Molly paused for a rest. "Walking lets you experience the countryside, that's for sure." Setting off again, she stumbled on the uneven ground and almost collided with a gorse bush.

"Careful. That's not the kind of experience you want." Carol grabbed her friend's arm and steadied her.

Fortunately, the rest of their journey back to the castle was uneventful. When they entered the lobby, Lady Freya greeted them. "Did you have a nice stroll?" she asked.

They told her about their afternoon, even pulling out gifts to show her, which their hostess admired graciously.

"What time is dinner?" Laura asked as she returned the plaid earmuffs to her bag. She was hoping she had time for a short nap.

"At seven," Lady Freya said. "Tonight we have a special reception for the television people, dinner included. You're welcome to join, but if you don't want to attend, I can serve you separately in a private room."

Catching sight of Molly's expression, Laura knew the correct answer. "We'd love to attend the reception. I presume we should dress up?" Anticipating that they might enjoy a fancy dinner together at least once, the friends had packed semi-formal outfits.

"A nice dress will do," Lady Freya said. "We'll see you at seven then?" She made a notation on what appeared to be a guest list.

The trio climbed the massive staircase, chattering about the evening ahead. Once upstairs, they each went to their rooms to rest for a couple of hours. Laura dashed off a quick text and a few photos to Brody, then lay down on the bed with a book. Within five minutes she was sound asleep, the book facedown on her chest.

The sound of her phone chirping with a text alert startled Laura awake, and at first she couldn't place where she was, let alone the time or day. *The castle. Dinner.* She needed to get ready. But first, she checked her phone and laughed out loud at Brody's response to her earlier message: *Don't send any more photos unless you want to accommodate stowaways. Adina and Henry are scheming to book flights to Scotland tonight.*

There was also a recent text from Carol asking if she was ready for dinner. She responded by urging her friends to go ahead without her. She took a quick shower, dried her hair, and applied some makeup to brighten her complexion. Dresses weren't her usual style, so she wore trim black pants and a plum-hued silk top with an asymmetrical neckline, then added heels and dramatic earrings.

When Laura stepped out of her room, the hallway was hushed, occasional electric sconces the only source of light. On an impulse, she decided to go downstairs a different way, via a staircase that would bring her closer to the ballroom where the reception was being held.

Relying only on her mental map, Laura took a corridor that branched off the main one. This hallway was slightly narrower, obviously built in an earlier time. All the doors she passed were closed, and no sounds penetrated the thick wooden doors.

The hallway went on and on. Had she gone the wrong way? The castle was a maze. She shrugged. If she didn't find the staircase soon, she would retrace her steps. And she did have her cell phone, so she could easily call for help if need be. She couldn't help but laugh at how absurd it would be to call downstairs and tell her friends she was lost in the same building.

About ten yards further down the corridor, she found the stairs at last. As Laura began to head down, though, a voice echoed up the stairwell.

"Why won't you listen to me?" a frustrated female voice was arguing. "When it all goes up in flames, don't say I didn't warn you."

5

Laura paused, not wanting to intrude on a personal conversation. She waited a few seconds before continuing down, but as she went, the couple—for she heard a man's voice too—stayed just the right distance ahead so that she could still hear most of their discussion. She thought the acoustics of the castle's architecture might have something to do with the clarity of their voices as well.

"Handle it the way you want," the woman said. "But if you don't take care of the situation, I'll have to get involved. I've worked too hard to see my career go down the drain."

"You're exaggerating," the man replied. "She's got a great deal and she knows it."

"Obviously not. She's going to quit, I tell you."

The man gave a scoffing laugh. "That would be career suicide."

Laura couldn't help but be curious. Who was going to quit? And who was so certain she wouldn't? Chiding herself that it was none of her business, Laura again stopped, this time on a landing. From here she could see the first floor below, and she spotted Clive and Kyla hurrying away.

They must be talking about their show's star, Charlotte. It sounded as though she wanted to quit the show, which was a surprise since it appeared successful and popular. *Molly would flip if she heard this!*

But not a word would leak from Laura's lips, not even to her best friends. Charlotte's business was her own, and the last thing Laura wanted to do was hurt someone by revealing private matters. Besides, it might not even be true. Rumors were always flying around about actors and actresses.

A panting sound announced the arrival of Minnie from behind Laura. "What are you doing here?" she asked the friendly creature, though keeping her distance from the dog's slobber-lined chops. "Can you show me the way to the ballroom?"

Minnie stared at her for a moment, then, as if she understood, pushed past Laura to thump the rest of the way down the stairs. At the very least, the dog would lead the way to her master, right? *Or her food dish. A dog after my own heart.*

At the foot of the staircase, Laura continued to follow Minnie. As they drew closer to a set of open double doors, the sound of conversation and light chamber music drifted her way. Nerves tingling, Laura stopped in front of a gilt-framed mirror for a last check, then met her friends inside the doorway.

Carol and Molly, both lovely in flattering cocktail dresses, broke into smiles when Laura entered. "There you are," Carol said. "We thought you got lost."

Laura laughed. "I almost did. I decided to try another staircase. But Minnie helped me find my way." She saw from the corner of her eye that the dog had located her mistress, who greeted her with delight.

"You'll have to show us when we go up to bed," Molly said. "I really want to learn my way around."

"We might need bread crumbs in a place this size." Carol shifted her gaze toward Lord and Lady Cameron, both in formal Highland garb. The regal couple stood in front of a massive fireplace greeting guests, their huge black dog sitting beside them. "Do you want to get into the receiving line?"

"I suppose we should," Laura said. "It's all part of the experience, right?"

As they approached their hosts, Laura saw that the room was quite full of people. Several faces were familiar from the film shoot they'd driven past, joined by others who, with their tattoos and stylish attire, were almost a different species than the locals. In contrast, the villagers had followed suit with the lord and lady and wore kilts, sporrans, and plaids. The effect was quite picturesque, as if they were all part of a television show tonight.

Another man stood beside Lady Freya, and as they joined the receiving line, Laura recognized him as the gentleman who had answered the door at the manor when Charlotte knocked.

"Lord Sebastian, I'd like you to meet our honored guest," Lady Freya said, gesturing to the next person in the queue. "This is Miss Charlotte Martin, star of *A Highland Lass.*"

Laura expected the pair to mention something about their earlier meeting, but to her surprise, Lord Sebastian bowed over Charlotte's hand and said, "It's a pleasure to make your acquaintance." Laura glanced at her friends, who appeared equally puzzled, then gave a mental shrug. Another observation that wasn't her business. Charlotte and the lord of the manor must have good reasons to pretend they hadn't met.

After a few minutes, it was the Americans' turn to say hello. "You look lovely tonight, ladies," Lady Freya said. "Lord Sebastian MacVail, I'd like to introduce you to our guests, here all the way from the States."

The nobleman expressed polite interest in this information and they all chatted for a moment about the trip to Scotland from Michigan.

"We were admiring your home when we took a walk this afternoon," Laura said. "It's a beautiful place."

Lord Sebastian tipped his head in acknowledgment. "Thank you. It's been in the family for generations. I feel most fortunate."

"As do we," Lady Freya said. "But we've only been here a few years. Alan inherited after his cousin passed."

"But you've done wonderful updates on the place already," Lord Sebastian said. "Many such properties are struggling to survive."

"It's a money pit all right," Lord Alan put in. "Thank goodness for my publishing success." He ran a finger around the inside of his collar and rolled his eyes in a gesture of relief.

"Alan writes Scottish police thrillers under a pen name, Barton Bruce," Lady Freya explained. "Not many people know that."

"Three more do now, my dear." Lord Alan pulled a face. "You're blowing my cover."

"Oh, my husband loves those." Carol put a hand to her mouth. "Would you autograph one for me?"

Lord Alan bowed, smiling. "That can be arranged. I have copies available here."

Carol practically jumped up and down. "A Scottish tam and now an autographed book? Harvey will be over the moon."

"That's what we aim for here at Glenellen Castle." Lady Freya beamed at them. "There's a village event coming up that you'll enjoy—a garden party at Glenellen Manor later this week."

"We're invited?" Now Laura felt like bouncing with joy. Beyond the cooking lessons and exploring the countryside, they were getting a taste of life in Glenellen. Speaking for the others, she said, "We'd love to go. Thank you."

There were others waiting to greet the hosts, so the trio moved along. The next stop was a buffet table, where hors d'oeuvres were laid out in an attractive display.

Finally hungry after their big lunch and snack, Laura surveyed the choices, trying to decide between mini sausage rolls, smoked salmon on tattie scones, smoked haddock balls, and Scotch eggs. This was in addition to platters heaped with crudités, gourmet cheeses, crackers, and fresh fruit. Laura's mouth watered over the array of cheeses, traditional selections including soft Highland crowdie, hard and aged Dunlop, and Caboc, a Scottish cream cheese.

"Oh my," Carol said, ferrying a loaded plate to a small table, where they all sat. "Everything looks so good."

"Think of it as research." Laura grinned. "I'm going to ignore calories until we get home."

"Good plan." Molly laughed. "Of course we can always do more walking to counteract our intake."

"We'd better." Carol raised an eyebrow. "Or else my luggage won't be the only thing that's overweight on the flight home."

Laura nibbled at her appetizers, watching the crowd with interest. She noticed how Finn circled the room almost in pursuit of Charlotte, only to have her elude him time and again.

"Charlotte and Finn used to date," Molly said quietly, apparently noticing what held Laura's attention. "At least according to the tabloids. They must have broken up."

"Is anything in the tabloids real?" Carol asked. "Don't they make up stories just to create buzz about people?"

Molly sliced open a Scotch egg, revealing the egg heart surrounded by ground meat. The outside was breaded and crispy. "I think they do sometimes. But there's got to be something wrong between those two. Why else would she keep avoiding him?"

"Maybe he's difficult to work with," Carol said, then held up a hand to forestall Molly's objection. "I know he's a dreamboat, as we used to say in the old days, but sometimes they're the worst."

Now the star was deep in conversation with Agnes, who looked lovely in traditional Scottish evening dress featuring a light green tartan. Under the glittering chandeliers, her chestnut updo glinted with rich highlights.

"I can't wait for tomorrow's baking lesson," Molly said. "Today was so much fun."

"I was impressed," Laura said. "You did really well despite your piecrust phobia."

The string quartet had now stopped playing, and Lady Freya clinked on a glass to get everyone's attention. "Please, everyone, keep enjoying the buffet. We'll be bringing out main dishes soon. But for now, welcome the Glenellen Dancers, accompanied by the Lads and Lassies of Loch Ellen."

Applause broke out as four men and four women in Cameron tartan entered the room, followed by six members of a folk group carrying their instruments. The dancers formed two lines while the band settled in.

"This is fun," Laura said, eager to see how the performance would compare to The Leaping Lowlanders and The Piping Yoopers, the dance and bagpipe groups they had in Loch Mallaig.

With a nod from the leader, the wail of a fiddle led off, joined by the beat of a bodhran, the drone of a bagpipe, and the bouncy notes of a concertina. The dancers began to move in a series of steps Laura recognized as "Castle in the Air," a frolic with much crossing back and forth, holding hands and turning, and stepping in place.

The onlookers were enthralled as the dancers performed several numbers. When the troupe took a final bow, applause rang out. Laura noticed that the director, Clive, beelined to talk to the performers and wondered if they'd strike a deal to appear in a future episode.

"Wasn't that great?" Molly grinned. "I really loved it."

"It was," Carol agreed. "I was pretending it was a couple hundred years ago and we were at a castle banquet."

"You're not far off." Laura pointed to catering employees dressed in white who were rolling out carts holding the main courses. One of the choices was an enormous roast, lifted carefully to the table by two men. She regarded her empty plate ruefully. "I'm not sure if I can stuff in another bite of food," she said, and the other two agreed with her about this sad state of affairs.

"Why don't we go out to the garden?" Carol suggested. "It's a warm night and I'd love to get some air."

The trio exited the castle through a line of French doors leading onto a terrace. The patio was enclosed with a low wall, urns holding topiaries at intervals, and on both ends, stairs went down to the lawn. Laura could picture couples cooling off between dances at balls held here long ago.

"This is a good place to sit." Laura perched on the wall, which still held warmth from the day. From here she could see through the trees to the glassy loch. Overhead, stars began to pop out in an indigo sky still shaded delicate green in the west. In a nearby tree, an owl hooted.

Molly inhaled a deep breath and released it slowly. "Oh, this is lovely."

They fell into a pleasant silence as they soaked in the atmosphere of the ancient building and gardens. Inside, people lined up at the buffet table, then sat to eat. But after a while Laura tuned that out, keeping her attention focused outward.

The rattle of a door handle startled her, and she glanced over to see Charlotte burst out of the ballroom, clutching a black velvet evening cloak at her neck. The actress didn't appear to notice them as she veered toward one of the staircases. "I've made a royal mess of it," she muttered, her head down as she navigated the steps. A minute or so later, Laura saw her figure winding through the trees. Soon, she was swallowed up in the dark woods.

The door rattled again, this time revealing the tall figure of Finn Paterson. He stood, hands on hips, and looked around. "Evening, ladies. Have you seen Charlotte?" he asked in his charming Scottish accent. "I need to talk to her."

"She went into the garden," Molly said, pointing. "Into the woods over there."

Finn peered in that direction then took off at a trot. "Thank you," he called back as he practically flew down the steps. Soon he was also lost to the night.

"That's so romantic," Molly said, a hand to her chest. "He's chasing her down to say he loves her."

Carol's brow creased. "I hope that's it. Maybe we shouldn't have said anything."

Molly scoffed. "Finn Paterson is harmless. He teaches reading to small children in his spare time."

That did sound commendable, but Laura couldn't help but share Carol's misgivings. Maybe the actress didn't want to talk to her costar. Then again, with the size and complexity of the castle gardens, she could probably easily avoid him. Especially at night.

Laura woke up early the next morning, refreshed and ready for the day. Padding across the carpet, she opened the curtains to reveal gorgeous sunshine and a blue sky with only a couple of puffy clouds sailing along.

She needed to be out there as soon as possible. After throwing on leggings, a long-sleeve running shirt, and sneakers, Laura grabbed her phone and headed out. She thought about texting the others to tell them where she was, but she didn't want the notification to wake them if they hadn't switched their phones off.

The castle was quiet too. Laura decided to go out through the terrace, so she took the back stairs and went into the ballroom. The vast room was dark, with the table and chairs neatly lined up and all traces of the festivities cleared away. What a wonderful night it had been. Laura hummed one of the songs quietly, hoping they'd have a chance to see the dancers again.

Birds sang in the trees beyond the terrace, welcoming the morning light. Laura trotted down the stone steps and onto a paved pathway. She decided to try the woods route down to the loch, which Terry had said was shorter.

She easily found the path, which wasn't much more than a beaten track. She jogged along, her pace unsteady as the trail wound between stands of trees towering overhead. Normally she'd be frustrated if she couldn't keep up a regular tempo on a run, but this enchanted setting—like something out of a child's storybook—made her forget such things. Here and there, bluebells bloomed in mossy clearings, and Laura stopped to take a few photographs to share with her mother.

Down toward the loch the path went, until she emerged on the grassy meadow at the water's edge. Should she follow the shore for a while? Laura checked the time. If she jogged about fifteen minutes then turned around, she would get back when breakfast started.

This morning, ducks and other waterfowl were foraging along the loch's shore, and Laura enjoyed trying to identify them. Their quacks and honks were quite entertaining too. Then she left them behind as the path wound upward, over the headland. She'd go as far as the height of land before going back, she decided.

She was taking a brief rest on the cliff, inhaling the bracing air off the water, when something below caught her eye. Cautiously, she edged closer to the drop-off, blinking as she stared down. Something black washed back and forth in the gentle waves quite a distance out, near an outcropping of rocks.

In an instant, Laura recognized the black fabric as Charlotte's cloak—and the lifeless actress was still wearing it.

6

Laura's knees buckled and she sank onto the grass, staring at the swirling fabric with horror. Was she mistaken? Had Charlotte simply dropped her cloak into the water? No, Laura knew she wasn't wrong. Charlotte was dead.

A whistle echoed across the field, followed by a shout. Laura glanced up to see a fluffy dog trotting toward her. Before she could react, he was upon her, sniffing at her face.

"He's harmless," a man said, and when Laura disentangled herself, she saw it was Lord Sebastian. "Like most bearded collies. His name is Mack."

Laura gave the dog a pat and pushed herself to her feet. "I'm glad you're here. Look." With a shaking finger, she pointed toward the water, unable to say more.

The lord sucked in a sharp breath. "Who is it? Do you know?" He fumbled in the pocket of his tweed coat and pulled out a phone.

"It's Charlotte Martin." A cold, swooping sensation overcame Laura and she sat again, facing away from the loch.

"There's been an accident," Lord Sebastian said into the phone, his voice shaking slightly. "A woman has fallen into the loch and drowned."

An accident was a reasonable assumption, especially if Charlotte had been walking along here in the dark. The footing was treacherous and the drop-off abrupt. But despite that logic, a note of warning chimed in Laura's mind. Had Charlotte fallen—or been pushed? She thought of Finn running after the actress and again felt a twist of guilt. Had they had an argument that resulted in Charlotte's death?

Laura leaned her forehead against her knees, trying to suppress the nausea churning in her belly. Then she patted her pocket and retrieved her own phone. She needed her friends and she needed them now.

Carol answered on the first ring. "Where are you? We're getting ready to go down to breakfast."

"I'm—" For a few seconds, Laura couldn't form the words. Then she blurted in a rush, "I went for a run near the loch. Charlotte Martin fell in. She's dead."

Carol gasped sharply. "Oh no. That's terrible. Where are you exactly? We'll be right there."

Laura explained where she was and hung up, grateful that she had such supportive friends.

"Are you all right?" The laird peered at her anxiously. "I'm sorry, but I don't remember your name."

"Laura Donovan," she said. "From America. Here for the cooking lessons."

"That's right," he said. "I'm Sebastian MacVail." His expression became rueful. "Terrible to meet again under such circumstances."

That's for sure. "Are the police coming soon?" Laura expected that they would want to talk to her, although she didn't know anything. Well, except that Finn had chased after Charlotte last night. And that the actress had supposedly wanted to quit the show, according to the conversation she'd overheard between Kyla and Clive. She remembered Charlotte had visited Sebastian too. Should she say anything to the laird about that? *No,* she realized with a grimace. Not until the police figured out what had happened.

Lord Sebastian was staring out over the water, his expression distant and somewhat foreboding. "What's that you asked? The police? They'll be here as soon as they can, though this isn't the most convenient spot."

He could say that again. There was no road access, so the authorities would have to come through the field or by water. Laura remained seated, watching as the dog explored the nearby bushes and clumps of tall grass.

Finally, two familiar figures came trudging along the path, Molly in the lead. Molly spotted her and waved, and the duo began to trot. By the time they reached her, Laura was standing, and the new arrivals engulfed her in a hug. "My friends," Laura explained to Lord Sebastian. "Molly and Carol." The collie came to investigate and Laura told them his name. Anything to distract herself from why she was still by the loch.

A buzzing sound announced the arrival of a boat owned by Police Scotland, as the force was called. One officer was at the helm, while three more were in the back, one dressed in a wet suit. The boat stopped offshore a good distance from the floating body, then the diver put on a mask and jumped overboard.

"The water is still terribly cold from the melting snow on the mountains," Lord Sebastian said.

His remark made Laura shiver. *Poor Charlotte. It must have been such a shock to fall into freezing water. Hopefully she didn't suffer long.*

The man in the wet suit swam over to the body, then he gestured for the boat to edge closer. Working together, they retrieved the body and carefully placed it in the boat. After conferring for a bit, the captain brought the boat to shore and two of the officers, a man and a woman, disembarked. The boat roared away while the officers climbed up a flight of stairs to the top of the cliff. Both wore black fleece jackets and trousers with neon vests and black hats with a checked band.

"Good morning," the man said. "I'm Inspector Gough and this is Constable Hail." His keen eyes examined each face while the constable prepared to take notes. "One of you called in regarding the victim?"

"I did." The laird raised his hand.

Gough gave him a nod of greeting. "Lord Sebastian. Are you the one who discovered her?"

"No, I was," Laura said. "I was taking a break from my run when I saw Charlotte Martin in the water. I'm Laura Donovan from Michigan. I'm staying at the castle with my friends."

Inspector Gough's gaze sharpened even further. "You knew the victim?"

Laura shifted from foot to foot. "I didn't really know her. I met her only yesterday, but I recognized her clothing. She was wearing that cloak last night."

"We saw her wearing it too," Carol said.

The inspector put up a hand. "Hold on, let us get your details." He held his questions until Carol and Molly gave their names. "Back to you, Ms. Donovan. What time did you first see the victim?"

Laura took them through her morning, estimating the time that she'd arrived at the top of the cliff. Lord Sebastian confirmed that he'd come along right after, walking the dog.

"Neither of you went down to the beach or attempted to rescue the victim?"

They confirmed that they hadn't. Laura didn't add that she'd known the woman was beyond help at first glance.

"Back to last night," the inspector went on. "What time did you see Ms. Martin wearing the cloak?"

"I'm not exactly sure," Laura said. "It was after the dance performance at the castle. We were on the terrace when she came outside and went down into the garden."

"Maybe around nine?" Carol guessed. "It was right as dinner was being served. Lady Freya can probably tell you. Unless you noticed, Lord Sebastian."

He shrugged. "I didn't, really. I was too busy digging into the roast beef. My, they put on a good spread."

"How did she seem to you?" the inspector asked Laura.

Laura recalled Charlotte's comment. "She said, 'I've made a royal mess of it,' but I don't know what she was talking about."

The constable dutifully took that down, then Inspector Gough asked the question Laura had been dreading. "Did you see anyone else go into the garden?"

Carol shifted position and Molly winced, signs they realized the question's importance. Laura squared her shoulders. She had to tell the truth. "Yes, we did. Finn Paterson came out on the terrace and asked if we'd seen Charlotte. We told him that she'd gone into the garden, and he followed her."

Although the officers were trained not to show emotion, Laura thought she saw them react to this news. No doubt they considered Finn's presence a solid lead to whatever had befallen the actress.

"Is there anything else you can tell me about last night?" the inspector asked.

Laura glanced at her friends, who shrugged. "No, I'm afraid not. Soon after we saw Finn, we went back inside for dinner, and then we went to bed. And like I told you, this morning I decided to take an early run along the loch. I didn't see anyone until Lord Sebastian and his dog showed up."

"And neither of you were out here this morning?" Gough asked Carol and Molly.

"No, not until Laura called us," Carol said. "She asked us for support and that's why we're here." She lifted her chin, as though daring the inspector to challenge her wanting to help a friend in need.

But Gough seemed to accept that. "How long are you staying at the castle?" When they told him their return date, he nodded in apparent satisfaction that they'd be available for more questioning if needed. "You can be on your way then. I'm sure you'll want to take it easy for a bit." His eyes were sympathetic as they rested on Laura.

"I am still a bit shaken," Laura admitted. She thought for a moment then, encouraged by his kind manner, went ahead and asked, "Do you think she fell into the water?"

Inspector Gough cleared his throat. "She may have, but that is not what killed her. She was strangled with the Cameron tartan scarf we found wrapped around her neck."

7

The inspector's words rang in Laura's ears the entire way back to the castle. Someone had used a Cameron scarf to murder Charlotte. A scarf in that plaid wasn't exactly an uncommon item in these parts. Not only did it belong to their hosts' clan, but the show used it too.

"That tartan certainly doesn't narrow it down any," Carol said, as if reading Laura's thoughts. "Even the gardener wears it." They were now on the castle grounds, and after a little hesitation, they decided to take the path through the woods. It was much shorter, if dark and steep.

"That's right," Molly said. "How are they ever going to figure it out?" The usually bubbly event planner sounded glum. "I for one can't believe Finn did such a thing. He cared about her too much."

Laura studied her friend with compassion, understanding that she was a fan grieving the death of a favorite actress—and suspicion had tarnished another television hero. "Me neither, but it doesn't look good for him at the moment. He might have been the last person to see her alive."

"Well, I sure hope they figure out who came along after him." Molly put her head down and picked up the pace, her sneakers thumping on the packed dirt.

Grateful for the bottled water Carol had brought her, Laura swallowed some before tackling the hill. She was light-headed with shock and hunger, and she hoped breakfast was still available. It was hard to believe she had an appetite considering the circumstances, but she assumed it was the exercise and fresh air.

They entered the castle through the side door and went first to the dining room. No one was in there eating, but Lady Freya was fussing over the buffet table. "There you are. I was just about to put this all away."

"We won't take long," Laura assured their hostess. "Sorry we're late. We were down by the loch."

"It's a beautiful morning, isn't it?" Lady Freya chirped, moving to the coffee urn to check the level.

Laura bit her lip. Should they tell their kind hostess what had befallen her guest? By the uneasy expressions on her friends' faces, they were wondering the same thing. Catching their eye, she shook her head slightly. The police would probably prefer to make the announcement.

"It is a gorgeous day," Laura agreed, pushing up her sleeves as she walked up to the table. She lifted the chafing dish lids. "Oh, scrambled eggs and sausage. Perfect."

"They should still be hot. If not, please let me know." Lady Freya tapped the top of the urn. "There's plenty of coffee left."

The doorbell chimed, sounding like the pull of a bell rope attached to a huge brass bell. Lady Freya's brow knit. "I wonder who that is. Please excuse me."

"Three guesses," Carol said under her breath as Lady Freya bustled out of the room. "Now we can stop pretending everything is fine."

Laura sighed and reached a hand up to knead the knot in her neck. "I'm not one for keeping secrets, but it wasn't up to us to break the news. The police probably like to see people's first reactions."

Molly shuddered. "I wouldn't want that job. Imagine having to give people bad news all the time." She scooped eggs onto a plate.

"Agreed." Laura used tongs to grab a sausage. "I'd rather feed them and make them happy."

Molly smiled. "It's an important job. Food is pretty essential to life, right?"

"It sure is." Carol picked up a small glass bowl and filled it with mixed fruit. "And it's one of life's chief pleasures too."

Terry, the gardener, appeared in the doorway but took a step back when he saw the women. "Sorry. I usually come up for my coffee break about now."

"Please come in," Laura said. "We're late today." She looked the gardener over, noticing that he wasn't wearing his tartan muffler today. "Finally warm enough to not wear a scarf?"

Busy dispensing coffee into a mug, the gardener pursed his lips. "I can't find my scarf. Must have misplaced it somewhere."

8

Terry's words hung in the dining room's hushed quiet. Laura bit her tongue, wishing she hadn't asked the question. She had a sickening idea where the scarf had ended up. The big question was, did Terry have anything to do with it?

Carol and Molly shared her concern, judging by the way they gathered up their plates and bowls and scurried to a table in the corner of the dining room.

Terry didn't seem to notice anything amiss. After doctoring his coffee, he wandered along to a platter of scones, where he carefully chose the perfect one.

Thoughts in a whirl, Laura finished serving herself breakfast. She shook her head when she realized she had put six sausages on her plate. Groaning to herself, she put four of them back, then joined the others. In a murder investigation, everyone was a suspect until cleared, even this kindly old gardener puttering around the dining room.

Voices drifted down the corridor, attracting Terry's attention. "I'd better go find out what Lady Freya wants me to do next," he said, shuffling toward the door. "Good day, ladies."

As soon as he was gone, Carol bent forward over the table. "Do you think that it was his scarf?"

Molly's features twisted in distress. "I sure hope not. I like Terry."

"Me too." Laura picked up a piece of toast and chewed, the hearty grain tasting like sawdust in her mouth. She wasn't going to enjoy this meal, but she'd better eat anyway. An empty stomach and light head wouldn't improve matters.

"I wonder if we'll have the baking lesson today," Carol said.

"Good question." Molly still sounded glum. "I don't feel right just going about my day as if this tragedy didn't happen."

"True, but sitting around isn't going to help us feel better," Laura countered.

"And the police seemed glad we'd still be around the castle for questioning," Carol added. "If we're going to be here and class is still being held, we might as well bake."

Laura tried to smile, but it felt unnatural on her face. "That should be my line. Baking has been therapy for many, many things in my life."

Molly sighed. "Let's hope it works today."

Despite trips to their rooms to shower and get dressed, the Bakehouse Three were first to arrive in the kitchen for their lesson. A kettle simmering on the AGA stove was the only sign of life. "Maybe we didn't get the memo," Carol said, setting her tote on the floor beside the counter. "Was class canceled after all?"

Molly checked her phone with a sigh. "I didn't get any messages."

Lady Freya hurried into the room, a worried expression creasing her pleasant features. "Sorry I'm late. I got caught up with some estate business."

That was an understatement. "We know about Charlotte," Laura said gently. "I was the one who discovered her while on a run this morning."

Lady Freya's mouth dropped open. "Oh, my dear. That is dreadful." She hurried to the stove. "I'll have hot tea in a jiffy."

"That would be nice, Lady Freya," Carol said. "But we were wondering, are we having a lesson today?"

Their hostess flipped the gas flame to high under the kettle. "We are. Agnes wasn't all that keen, but I didn't want to disappoint you. Kyla will be sitting in and so will I."

"Finn's not coming?" Molly asked, her eyes wide.

Laura expected Lady Freya to say that the actor had been arrested. But instead her ladyship said, "He's gone to Edinburgh. He left last night." She pulled open a tea tin to check the contents.

Left or fled? "Is he coming back?" Laura found herself asking.

Lady Freya paused in the act of scooping tea leaves into a teapot. "Why wouldn't he? There will be all kinds of meetings now about the show." She resumed her task. "They just completed filming the last episode, thankfully. Everyone was still here in case reshoots were needed."

"Do you think there will be a third season now?" Molly asked. She perched on a stool at the counter. "I can't imagine anyone taking Charlotte's place."

"She is a tough act to follow." Lady Freya carried over the teapot, then busied herself retrieving a sugar bowl and pouring milk into a small pitcher.

Laura found mugs on a shelf and brought over half a dozen. Both Molly and Lady Freya made good points. If someone from the show had killed Charlotte because she was leaving, then they had only hurt themselves. Maybe she could have been convinced to stay. But perhaps her death had nothing to do with the show at all. Interpersonal conflict was a strong possibility.

That thought brought her back to Finn. It didn't look good for his innocence that he'd left the property.

Footsteps on the flagstone floor announced the instructor's arrival.

With locks of hair trailing from her bun and her cardigan buttoned wrong, Agnes was far from her usual tidy self. Her face was set in grumpy lines as well.

"Time to get to work," she said without preamble. Not waiting for a response, she went to a closet and pulled out bib aprons. "How many today, Lady Freya?"

"Five," Lady Freya said. "Kyla should be here any moment."

As if summoned by the mention of her name, the sound of running feet echoed in the corridor and Kyla burst though the doorway. She also appeared out of sorts, her hair tangled and her shirttail hanging out of her jeans. "How are you all doing?" She moved around the room and hugged each woman, even Agnes, who submitted with great reluctance. "Isn't it awful about Charlotte? I'm so upset."

But despite the tears shining in Kyla's eyes, her dramatic sniffing and nose blowing, Laura sensed the actress didn't mind the drama. Then she chided herself for this uncharitable thought. *Maybe I'm reading too much into things. Just because Kyla was at odds with Charlotte, it doesn't mean she's not mourning Charlotte's death.*

Agnes didn't let them stay somber for long. "Finish your tea and wash up, ladies. We're making oatmeal bread today."

After washing their hands and donning aprons, the group worked together to lug containers from the pantry to the work area and to gather bowls, spoons, and measuring utensils. Laura found comfort in the familiar tasks.

"This recipe is a classic," Agnes said, using her TV personality voice. "Hearty and dense, it's perfect slathered with homemade butter and jam or local honey."

"After our loaves bake, we can try them with a bowl of the Scotch broth Mrs. Beasley made last night," Lady Freya added.

"Yum," Carol said. "I love Scotch broth."

The hearty soup's ingredients usually included lamb shank, barley, turnips, and peas, though these could be changed based on the cook's preferences. Laura enjoyed it too, and maybe after a couple of hours she would regain her appetite. Right now she was still stuffed from breakfast.

The first step was to proof the yeast, a process Laura had always found fascinating. A little sweet liquid and the dry powder came back to life, bubbling and frothing.

"Normally I use a stand mixer for bread," Agnes said. "But today we're going to use our muscles. I often find that a little beating and kneading does wonders for my psyche." She twitched her lips in a rare smile.

Let's hope it works. Although she had plenty of practice making bread, Laura followed Agnes's instructions closely, adding flour and oatmeal to the bowl holding the yeast. Honey and a little oil and salt completed the recipe. Then it was time to knead the dough until it was elastic and smooth. As they worked, Agnes lectured them on the science of yeast bread.

Laura channeled her tension into kneading the dough, putting every bit of her strength into it. All her questions, doubts, and fears went into that pummeled lump. *Careful,* she cautioned herself. *The last thing you need is for your idol to think you're an amateur who over kneads her dough.*

"Do this every day and you'll never have to lift weights," Molly said, a bit of cheer returning to her voice.

"Now we know why Laura's so buff," Carol said with a smile.

Laura poked her dough to see if it sprang back, then plopped it into a greased bowl and covered it with a cloth.

"All right, everyone," Agnes said after all the students had put their dough in bowls to rise. "Take a break. See you back here in an hour."

"What do you want to do?" Molly asked, taking off her apron. "Maybe go get some fresh air in the garden?"

Carol waved her phone. "I'm going to give Harvey a call. He should be awake by now."

"I'll go for a stroll with you, Molly," Laura offered.

The afternoon was warm enough that they didn't need jackets. With Minnie trotting at their heels, Laura and Molly went out the front door to explore some gardens on the other side of the castle. Here, a well-tended gravel path wound through rhododendron and azalea hedges, all coming into bloom.

"Isn't this gorgeous?" Molly stopped to take a picture of the colorful blossoms. Minnie, panting with enthusiasm, seemed to agree.

Laura tipped back her head and gazed at the clear sky, even bluer against sprays of white blossoms from an apple tree. "It really is." The restful beauty of the garden soaked into her spirit in much the way the sun's heat was baking her to her bones.

They strolled along in silence, not wanting to disturb the peace with discussion of the tragedy. After the hedges ended, they found themselves walking along the drive, where huge trees made a tunnel of green. They were admiring an ancient oak when Minnie lifted her head and sniffed the air before bolting down the road, moving faster than Laura thought possible due to the dog's bulky build.

"I wonder what that was about," Molly said.

"I have no idea," Laura said. "Maybe she smelled an animal."

"I suppose Minnie will be all right." Molly shrugged. "Lady Freya lets her roam freely, after all."

As they skirted a curve, Laura spotted Minnie standing next to a parked red Audi sedan. A figure sat in the driver's seat, unmoving.

Laura halted, grabbing her friend's arm. "Molly, who is that?"

Molly squinted, staring at the car. "I can't tell. The reflection off the windshield is blocking the view." Her face paled. "Do you think they're okay?"

"I sure hope so, but we'd better go check." With Molly right behind her, Laura made her leaden feet move forward, dreading what she would find with every step.

As they drew nearer, Laura heard sobs coming through the open driver's side window. Minnie paced outside the car, whining in response. Once they were close enough, Laura recognized Finn Paterson. He sat back in his seat, hands clutching the dark curls at his temples.

"Finn?" Laura said gently. "Are you all right?"

He lowered his hands and glanced up, revealing red-rimmed eyes. He blinked. "Do I know you?"

"We're guests at the castle," Laura said. "We did the baking class together yesterday."

And we know that you followed Charlotte into the garden. Laura shivered. Was it wise to be alone with the man if he was guilty of Charlotte's murder? That was an easy question to answer.

Laura began to back away. "Come on, Molly. Let's leave the man in peace."

"Wait," Finn said. "Now I remember you. You were on the terrace last night."

Uh-oh. Laura flexed her knees, ready to run. They were witnesses to his movements and he didn't know they'd already told the police.

But then the actor's handsome features twisted in agony. "Tell me—is it really true? Is Charlotte *dead*?" His deep voice cracked on the last word.

Laura inhaled a deep breath. "I'm afraid it is, Finn." She put up her hands, warding off potential questions. "But you'll have to ask the police for details."

He shook his head. "I don't want details." His face collapsed, revealing a glimpse of how he might look as a much older man. "When the reporters shouted the news at me, back at the gate, I hoped I was hearing wrong." He shuddered. "But I knew I wasn't. I had the worst feeling when I left last night . . ."

"The press is here already?" Molly asked. "Wow. That was fast."

Laura wasn't exactly surprised. A high-profile and untimely death was front-page news indeed. No doubt someone in the village had leaked it to the press. But she was more interested in following up on his remark about the previous evening. "What do you mean, you had a feeling?"

Finn rested both hands on the steering wheel, his expression thoughtful. "It's hard to put a finger on it, exactly. I tried to get her to come back to the castle with me, but she refused." Pressing his lips together, he shook his head. "I should have insisted."

"Did you see anyone else in the garden?" Laura asked. "Or down by the loch?" She wasn't sure why, exactly, but she believed Finn. Of course he could be acting, playing the role of bereaved suitor.

He tapped his fingers on the wheel, frowning. "No. Though I did hear something crashing around in the woods. But it was probably an animal."

Maybe not. But Laura didn't comment, not wanting to make Finn feel even worse about leaving Charlotte. Before she could think of something else to say, a Police Scotland car painted lime green, blue, and white came zipping down the road.

Laura recognized Inspector Gough behind the wheel as he stopped the car. He got out, as did his passenger, an older man equally as imposing as Gough.

"Good day, ladies," Gough said with a nod, then asked, "Who's that in the car?"

Finn opened his door and got out. "I'm Finn Paterson." He squared his shoulders. "I understand you'd like to talk to me about Charlotte Martin."

If Gough was surprised at the forthright admission, he didn't let on. "Yes we would, Mr. Paterson. This is Detective Inspector Wilson, now in charge of the case."

"Shall we meet at the castle?" Finn's lips lifted in a brief smile. "I promise I won't run off."

"That would be fine," Wilson said. "Go ahead and we'll follow."

The officers waited for Finn to get into his car and set off up the drive, then they trailed him closely in their vehicle.

"Want to turn around?" Molly asked. "I think we've walked far enough."

"Sure," Laura said. She consulted her phone for the time. "Yikes. We'd better hurry or we'll be late for class. Agnes will probably make us do all the dishes." With a laugh, the two women set off, arms and legs pumping. Minnie ran beside them, panting merrily all the way.

Two more police cars buzzed past as they walked, and when the women entered the castle, they saw a team of officers swarming up the main staircase. Just beyond the check-in desk, Constable Hail was closing the double doors to the drawing room, where the detective inspector and Finn were already seated. The interview was beginning.

Lord Alan hovered by the front desk. "They're here to search Charlotte's room. And it looks like Finn Paterson is under suspicion," he said, appearing bewildered by this latest turn of events. "What is this world coming to?"

"I don't have a good answer for that," Laura said. Seeing the man was tottering on his feet, she took his arm. "Do you want to sit down?" She guided him to a nearby settee. When he practically collapsed into the seat, she gazed at him with concern. "Do you want us to find Lady Freya?"

"She's upstairs," Lord Alan said. "Letting the officers into Charlotte's room. Please don't fuss. This death has really knocked me off my pins, but I'll be all right." He pulled out a handkerchief and mopped his brow. "It's one thing to study murder and mayhem from the safety of your desk chair. It's quite another to experience it."

Laura appreciated the truth of this remark. "Well, if you're sure you're all right, we'll leave you be. We're late for our baking lesson." Laura followed Molly out of the great hall, glancing back at the man who sat stricken on the settee. She prayed answers would be found soon, to bring justice for Charlotte and restore peace to the castle.

9

Mrs. Beasley and Agnes were whispering together by the ovens when the ladies entered the kitchen. They broke apart, Mrs. Beasley with a sniff and Agnes with a flush of embarrassment.

"Is it that time already?" Agnes asked, peering at the wall clock.

"I think so," Laura said, peeking under the cloth covering her bowl. Her dough had doubled in size.

Carol entered, pocketing her phone with the same half smile she always wore after talking to her husband. Laura grinned at her.

Agnes moved briskly toward the worktable. "Let's continue, then." She glanced around. "Where are Lady Freya and Kyla?"

"Lady Freya is busy with the police," Laura said on her way to the sink to wash up. "Not sure about Kyla."

The instructor's brow creased, but she didn't comment. Mrs. Beasley sniffed again as she pulled a soup pot out of the refrigerator. "That's what comes of letting all sorts stay here," she muttered, and Laura guessed she meant show business people.

Once again, Kyla tore into the kitchen at a run. "Sorry I'm late." She flapped the front of her top to cool down. "I had to help that dreamy Inspector Gough."

Laura agreed that the tall, dark policeman was handsome, but she wondered how dreamy Kyla would find the inspector once she learned he and his colleagues were grilling her brother as a potential suspect.

"What's going on?" Agnes asked, finally unbending enough to ask questions. "I saw several more police cars arrive."

Kyla reached for a towel to dry her hands. "They're looking for Charlotte's cell phone. I guess they didn't find it in her room." She beamed with pride. "But I was able to give them a description. It has a hot-pink alligator case."

Laura made a mental note. Cell phones were probably invaluable as evidence, since they basically held all the details of people's lives.

"All right, everyone," Agnes said. "Let's begin." She waited for Kyla to get to her station. "We're going to shape the loaves and let them rise again." She pulled the cloth from Lady Freya's bowl. "I'll do her ladyship's loaves to demonstrate."

Agnes had them prepare two loaf pans, then dump out their dough onto a floured surface and cut it in half. Then they shaped each section into loaf-like forms as Agnes instructed and placed them in the pans. Once again, the pans were covered and set to rise.

"That was easier than I thought," Molly said, sounding relieved.

Laura inspected Molly's work and smiled. The loaves were beautifully rounded and, if all went well, should turn out perfectly. "They look great. I think I might have competition in the Bread on Arrival kitchen soon."

Molly barked a laugh that caught a sharp glance from Agnes, then briefly covered her mouth with her hand. "I don't think you have anything to worry about."

"So, what shall we do now?" Laura asked. "Take another walk?"

"How about a cup of tea?" Carol suggested. "I think Lady Freya keeps hot water in the urns all day."

"You're becoming a real Scot," Molly teased as they made their way to the dining room. "Tea at all hours."

"And in all circumstances," Carol added. "It is comforting. I might keep up the habit at home."

"Speaking of home, how's Harvey?" Laura asked. "Is he lonely?"

Carol laughed. "Not with Angus around. They're two peas in a pod." She paused. "I didn't tell him about Charlotte. Maybe it's wrong of me, but he would just worry."

They were carrying mugs of tea out to the terrace when Detective Inspector Wilson entered the room, followed by Constable Hail.

"Excuse me, but I'd like to speak to you both," the detective said. Looking at Molly, he added, "Sorry, I didn't get your name."

"I'm Molly Ferris, Laura's business partner and friend," she answered. "And this is Carol MacCallan, our other partner."

"Do you want to talk to us separately or together?" Laura asked. She guessed he wanted to ask them what Finn had said out in the driveway.

"I think separately." He nodded at Laura. "You also found the deceased, correct?"

"I did." Laura fought back a sigh. She would naturally be first, then, as the witness with more to say. "I'll see you in a bit," she told her friends.

Cradling her mug, Laura trailed the officers back to the drawing room, where there was no sign of Finn. Hail closed the doors while Laura and the detective inspector got settled, then the constable perched on a chair to take notes.

"Let me know when you're ready, Ms. Donovan," the detective said.

Laura shifted in her seat. "Go ahead." She noticed that the blue eyes under beetling gray brows were quite kind.

He consulted a notepad resting on the table. "I understand you discovered the deceased. Can you take me through that, please?"

Once again, Laura gave her movements from the moment of waking up to her terrible discovery in the loch.

"Lord Sebastian came along when?" he asked.

Laura mentioned that his dog had approached first, and she'd watched the laird come across the field toward where she was sitting. She thought of several things she could add, including that she hadn't seen anyone else, but bit her lip, not wanting to muddy the waters with unnecessary details.

"All right then," Wilson said. "Let's move on to Finn Paterson. What happened this afternoon in the driveway?"

Laura explained how she and Molly were taking a walk during a class break and came upon the actor in the car. She relayed the conversation best as she could, especially the part where he asked if Charlotte was really dead. "He said the press gave him the news," she concluded. *Of course he said that*, a voice jeered in her head. *He wouldn't claim firsthand knowledge.* She ordered the voice to pipe down.

Wilson gave a gentle snort that conveyed what he thought of the media. "And I understand you saw Mr. Paterson last night, looking for the deceased?"

Laura squirmed, knowing this was very incriminating—in fact, it could be the key to the crime. Having such power made her uneasy. "Yes we did, all three of us. We were sitting out there enjoying the evening when Charlotte—Ms. Martin—came outside."

"Did she say anything?" This was a question Inspector Gough hadn't asked, though Laura had told him about what the actress had said.

"She muttered something to herself," Laura said. "I'm quoting the best I can: 'I've made a royal mess of it.'"

"How did she seem to you? Her mood, her demeanor."

Laura thought back, trying to remember the scene exactly. "Fine. I mean, a little upset—at herself, apparently—but not afraid or anything. We figured she wanted to get some air or be alone." She took a sip of tea, trying to ease her dry throat.

"And Mr. Paterson? How was he?"

The questions were calmly delivered but relentless, and Laura couldn't wait for the ordeal to be over. She described the actor's words and movements as well as she could.

"One more thing." The detective inspector shifted in his seat. "You haven't come across Ms. Martin's cell phone by chance, have you? It has a pink alligator skin case."

Laura shook her head. "I haven't seen it, but if I do, I'll call you immediately."

"Good, good." Wilson scanned his notes. "Is there anything else you can think to tell me? Any detail, no matter how slight, can be critical."

She immediately thought of Terry's scarf and was framing the words to mention it when Constable Hail's phone rang. She listened for a moment before passing the phone over to Wilson. "You'll want to hear this."

Wilson rose to his feet, listening intently. "A tip you say? An eyewitness saw them together?" He groaned. "Anonymous. Afraid to give their name, are they? But they said he owns the scarf?" Without another word to Laura, he motioned to Hail. "Let's go."

The pair bolted from the room, joined in the lobby by other officers streaming from various parts of the castle.

Behind the desk, Lady Freya glanced up from her work in alarm. "What's going on?" she asked. "Have you found the culprit?"

Detective Inspector Wilson didn't directly answer the question. Instead he asked, "Where might we find Terry, the gardener?"

10

Lady Freya put a hand to her mouth with a gasp. "You can't possibly think—" Visibly forcing herself to calm down, she said, "Out in the topiary garden, I expect. He was half an hour ago, anyway."

The officers conferred, then split into two or three groups and exited the castle. Laura sank onto a nearby chair, stunned by this turn of events.

Lady Freya came around the desk and sat in an adjacent chair. "A terrible mistake is about to be made," she said, wringing her hands. "Terry would never hurt anyone, not even a fly."

Though she didn't know the gardener well, Laura couldn't imagine him as the killer. Was the use of his scarf deliberate, to frame him? She was still mulling this over when Carol and Molly hurried into the lobby.

"What's going on?" Carol asked. "We saw officers in the garden."

"They've gone to arrest Terry," Lady Freya announced. "They think he killed that poor actress."

"So it was his scarf," Molly said. She perched on a sofa, joined by Carol. "I wondered why they didn't come get me for questioning."

"We were just finishing up when they got a call," Laura said. "A tip came in from someone who said they saw Terry with Charlotte last night."

"A tip?" Lady Freya drew back. "Did the police say who called it in?"

"I gathered it was anonymous," Laura said. "But they have to have more than that, right?" Maybe the scarf was enough to take him in.

"I have no idea," Carol said. "But he should get an attorney."

Lady Freya jumped to her feet. "Thank you, Carol. I've been sleeping on the job. I'd better call our solicitor." She darted behind the desk, where she lifted the receiver and began to dial.

"Why don't we go back to the kitchen?" Laura suggested, wanting to give Lady Freya some privacy. "Our bread must be about ready to go in."

"I forgot all about it," Carol admitted, rising to her feet with a groan. "Baking seems so unimportant right now."

Molly gasped, feigning shock at her friend's remark. "Baking is never unimportant. Plus it will give us something to do while we wait and fret."

The trio headed back to the kitchen, where Agnes was checking the ovens. "Just in time," she said. "We're up to temp and ready to roll."

Under the instructor's watchful eye, they slid their loaves into the ovens. Then Agnes set a timer. "When this rings, we'll check the loaves with a digital thermometer to ensure they are done."

Laura smiled but didn't say anything. With all her experience, she had the timing down to a science and could tell by looking at it if a baked good was ready. But her smile drooped as she thought of what her grandmother might say: *pride comes before a fall, Laura Elizabeth.*

Agnes set the timer down on the worktable. "I must apologize. I had a lecture prepared so we could make the most of the waiting time between stages. But today I find I am too distracted." She peered at them as though trying to judge their reaction. "I'll make it up to you over the next few days, I promise."

"Don't worry about it," Molly said. "We're all distracted today. Right now I couldn't absorb another bit of information if I tried."

Agnes appeared relieved. "Well, I'll see you back here in thirty-five minutes. Then you'll be able to sample the results of your hard work and Mrs. Beasley's soup." Pulling a cell phone out of her apron pocket, she headed out of the kitchen.

"Now we wait again." Carol laughed. "More tea?"

"Sure," Laura said. "I never finished my first cup." She thought guiltily of the mug sitting in the drawing room where she'd forgotten it in all the commotion of the anonymous tip.

They were dunking tea bags into mugs when Lady Freya entered the dining room. "Ah, there you are." She glanced around the room then into the hall before shutting the door. "I have something to ask you."

The Bakehouse Three exchanged glances, then Carol spoke for them. "Please, go ahead."

Lady Freya pulled out a chair at their table and sat. "I got hold of my solicitor and he's heading to the station to represent Terry. So that's good news." Taking a deep breath, she clasped her hands. "I get the sense that you ladies have a knack for handling these situations."

Laura wrinkled her brow. What situations did their hostess mean?

Lady Freya hunched her shoulders with a wince. "I hope this won't be too much of an imposition. But when you mentioned that your little town is like a miniature Scotland, I got curious, and I did some poking around on the Internet. What I found was a news article that indicated you three solved a murder case a little while ago."

Laura slid her eyes toward Carol and Molly, not sure how to respond. By their confounded expressions, she guessed they felt the same way she did. When they didn't respond, Laura said, "I admit we did end up investigating a murder. But it was kind of by accident. We certainly didn't set out with that intention."

"Of course not," Lady Freya said. "Just like we had no plans for one of our guests to get killed." Her face sagged with sadness. "But I feel it's the least we can do for poor Charlotte. I don't want whoever did this to get away with it."

The ladies murmured agreement. "And you don't believe Terry is responsible?" Carol asked.

Lady Freya shook her head. "No. And not just because I've known him forever. He's a gentle soul, content to spend his time making the gardens beautiful. I've never even seen him lose his temper."

"Never?" Molly probed. "He's always good-natured and calm?"

"That's right," their hostess confirmed. "Oh, he gets annoyed when black spot or insects attack the roses. But with another person? Never." She leaned forward across the table, urgency in her tone. "I'm afraid there's going to be a terrible miscarriage of justice. Please help us."

Laura and her friends exchanged glances. "All right, Lady Freya. We'll do our best. But we can't promise anything. We're not trained detectives."

Lady Freya slapped her palm on the table. "But you're experienced in reading people and figuring out what makes them tick. Am I wrong?"

"No, you're not wrong." Laura thought about the varied experience each of them had gained over decades of life and work. She'd dealt with her share of pressure in the restaurant world. As a former event planner, Molly had handled all sorts of personalities. And Carol was a former high school teacher, so if anyone was qualified to understand human nature, it was her. "We'll do our best, Lady Freya, I can promise you that."

Lady Freya rose from her seat. "That's all I can ask."

Carol glanced at her watch. "I believe the timers are about to go off. Shall we rescue the bread?"

Molly lifted her mug. "Drink up."

Their hostess paused in the doorway. "One more thing. Do you remember me telling you about the students who were ill? They will be here tomorrow." She clasped her hands. "Since the contract doesn't allow for refunds, they insisted on attending the remaining classes. I do hope . . ." With a low groan, she opened the door and escaped, leaving unsaid what she hoped, though Laura could guess. On top of the horror of Charlotte's death and Terry's probable arrest, both highly upsetting, the reputation of the castle hotel was at stake.

Carol shook her head. "Poor Lady Freya. She's really in a difficult spot."

"I'll say." Molly swallowed the last of her tea. "Good thing we're here to help her."

Laura hoped they would succeed. One solved case didn't exactly make them experts.

The bread was perfect—crusty and brown with a dense yet tender crumb. At least that was how Agnes described it in her television voice, waxing almost poetic as the students sliced into their loaves. They ate lunch right there in the kitchen, enjoying large bowls filled with steaming Scotch broth and thick slices of bread slathered with creamy butter.

"Yum," Molly said, taking another bite. "This is one of the best meals I've ever had." She took out her phone and snapped a picture of the remains of her loaf, which sat on a cutting board nearby. Then she took one of her pottery bowl, which had a slice resting on the rim. "These will be perfect shots for our social media page. Lots of our customers have been commenting on the photos I've posted so far, wishing they were here."

Carol waved a spoon at her. "That's why you're in charge of marketing. You whip up excitement while Laura whips up new recipes."

Laura grinned at Carol. "And your level head keeps us from whipping ourselves into a frenzy."

Lady Freya returned to the kitchen pushing a cart holding full bus pans, Mrs. Beasley behind her with the same. The Scotch broth and other dishes had been set out in the dining room for the film crew staying at the castle. Kyla must have eaten with them, because her slightly misshapen loaf sat on the counter, uncut.

"I'm glad you're still here, Agnes," Lady Freya said to the instructor, who was tapping away at a laptop across the room. "I have news."

Agnes peered over the top rim of her glasses. "What is it, Lady Freya? I made an exception for low numbers once, but I cannot continue."

Laura experienced a lurch of alarm, but then, remembering Lady Freya's earlier news, she felt a smile break across her face. The lessons were saved.

Lady Freya unloaded a tub of dishes in the dishwashing area. "The classes are full again, Agnes. The rest of the students have recovered from their illness and will be here tomorrow morning. Starting the lesson after lunch will be the only concession needed."

The instructor's mouth formed an O of dismay, but seeing that Laura and the others were watching, she clamped her lips shut. Then with a twitch of her shoulders, she turned back to her computer to tap at the keys.

Agnes wanted to cancel, Laura realized with disappointment. Yes, it was understandable under the circumstances. Many people would flee after a tragic death—once the police allowed them to. Did Agnes have another reason to cut the session short, besides it getting off to a bad start? Was she really just teaching this class for the paycheck, and therefore happy to get paid without having to do any work for it? Laura shook her head, not wanting unpleasant thoughts about one of her idols to creep into her mind.

After the meal, Mrs. Beasley shooed them away, refusing to let them help clean up. The three friends went out to the garden for a walk—and to decide how to approach the mission Lady Freya had given them.

"Where do we begin?" Laura asked her friends as they strolled. The castle was quiet now, the calm after the storm. Several cars, including Finn's red Audi, were in the parking area, so the film crew had to be around somewhere.

"I think we should write down all the suspects, their movements, and possible motivations," Carol said.

"Good idea," Molly agreed. "I'm going to dive into the tabloids. I can use my phone to access digital archives."

Laura smiled at her friend. "For research purposes, I'm guessing?"

Molly bent to smell a ruffled pink rose. "You bet. Oh, a lot of the stories are made up, but there could be nuggets of the truth somewhere. And I'll check out the film trades and regular newspapers too." She gestured, still cupping the blossom. "Smell this. It's heavenly."

They all agreed the rose scent was wonderful. Farther on, they spotted Kyla seated on a stone bench in the shade of a blooming hawthorn tree. She was playing with her phone, oblivious to the white petals drifting down to spangle her hair and the bench.

The crunch of a sneaker on the gravel path made her look up. Her expression wasn't exactly welcoming, but Laura decided to bluff her way through anyway.

"Hi, Kyla," she said with a wave. "Your bread is ready, by the way."

The actress put a hand to her mouth. "Whoops. I forgot all about it."

And no wonder, with her fellow castmate being killed. Once they drew a little closer, Laura said, "I'm sorry for your loss." Carol and Molly echoed the condolences.

"Thank you." Kyla bit her lip and looked down at her lap. "We weren't exactly friends, but I'll miss her."

"I'll bet," Laura said as the ladies perched on other benches in the grouping. "All of you must be pretty tight-knit."

Kyla made a face. "Some of us more than others. Finn and Charlotte dated for a while, from before the show even started filming.

I wondered how it would be on set after they broke up, but it was fine. I guess their relationship fizzled out."

That's not what Laura had observed, but she didn't say as much. "That must have been a relief."

"You could say that." Kyla pursed her lips in a rueful expression. "Finn wasn't serious anyway. He'll have a new girlfriend within the month, mark my words."

Judging by what the women had seen, this was such a blatant lie that Molly opened her mouth to object. Anticipating this, Laura touched her friend's arm. "Molly is a big fan of your show. And we're all looking forward to seeing the new episodes when they air."

"We have lots of fans," Kyla said with a shrug, dismissing their interest. "I hate to say it, but no publicity is bad publicity." She held up her phone, her eyes gleaming. "I have tons more likes on my posts now. Some fans are saying I should be the new star."

A twig cracked in the nearby woods. Laura glanced over her shoulder but didn't see anything. A squirrel? Maybe even a deer? Brushing off a sense of unease, she turned back to the conversation.

Carol lifted one brow. "They're going to replace Charlotte so quickly?" At Kyla's frown, she added, "Forgive me, I have no idea how these things work."

"What line of work are you in?" Kyla asked.

"I run a bakehouse with Molly and Laura now, but I used to teach high school math," she answered.

"Well there you go," Kyla said. "If a teacher called in sick, didn't they put in a substitute?"

"I suppose so," Carol said. "You can't leave a class unattended."

The snapping noise came from the woods again, and all three of the older women glanced over.

Kyla didn't give any sign she'd noticed. Instead, she went on, her voice eager. "You can't have a show without stars. So if Clive is on the ball, he'll get on that. It's time for me to be in the spotlight. I've worked hard for the opportunity."

But did you kill for it? Taken aback by the young woman's blatant self-absorption, especially under such tragic circumstances, Laura rose to her feet. "We'll be on our way. Good luck with the show."

Kyla was already busy on her phone, chuckling to herself. She flapped a hand in what was probably meant to be a wave.

Once they were well away from the spot, in a secluded area in the woods, the women let out gasps of disbelieving laughter.

"What a little twit," Carol said. "She has no empathy at all for her friend."

Molly frowned. "I don't think they were friends. More like rivals. Although Kyla could hardly play the female lead with Finn being her brother."

"I wonder if she'll try to push him out too," Laura said. "I heard her telling Clive that Charlotte was going to quit."

"When was that?" Molly asked, her expression avid. "Believe me when I say that Charlotte was the real star of that show, no matter what Kyla thinks. Charlotte leaving would have blown a hole in it."

Beyond where they had stopped was a mossy meadow filled with a carpet of bluebells. In awe of the gorgeous sight, Laura stepped over a fallen log to get closer to the flowers. The others picked their way off the path to the meadow as well. As they went, Laura told them the conversation she'd overheard on her way to the reception. "Kyla was warning Clive about it."

"So she threw her colleague under the bus," Carol mused. "How did he react?"

"He didn't seem to believe her," Laura said. "He thought Charlotte would be committing 'career suicide,' as he put it."

Carol's eyes widened. "Maybe Charlotte did tell Clive that she was leaving and he killed her in a rage."

Laura crouched among the bluebells and sniffed the light, delicate scent. "Could be. Or Kyla did away with her. She certainly seemed pretty cold-blooded about betraying Charlotte to her boss."

"With a friend like that, who needs enemies?" Contempt colored Carol's face. "I guess we have an entry for my suspect chart."

"We ought to track down Clive next," Molly said. "And talk to Finn again." She shivered. "I never thought I'd be trying to figure out who killed a TV star, or that half the main suspects would also be celebrities, no less."

"I think we need to remember that they are just people, even if they do have glamorous jobs," Laura warned. "That said, I have a hard time believing Finn is guilty, and it isn't because of his looks."

"I agree," Molly said. "He seemed genuinely upset when we came across him beside the road. In shock, almost."

"Could you tell me what happened again?" Carol requested. After Laura and Molly relayed the conversation as closely as they could, Carol nodded. "The police must believe him since they arrested Terry instead."

"Well, they had more proof against Terry," Laura pointed out. "Although we all agree that Finn is probably innocent, we really should keep an open mind."

Molly sighed. "Yes, you're right." She brightened. "I wonder if he has proof that clears him. Maybe I can question him and find out."

Carol and Laura laughed at her excitement about talking to the handsome star. "That will be on the list," Carol promised. "Establish alibis for all."

Something rustled in the bushes, and the sound was followed by the crunching of sticks underfoot. Alarmed, the three women froze in place. Was someone following them?

11

"What's out there?" Molly asked, her eyes wide. "Is it whatever—or whoever—made that noise earlier?"

"So creepy," Carol said with a shiver. "I thought maybe someone was listening when we talked to Kyla."

Laura frowned. Was someone stalking them? Then the bushes parted and a familiar creature trotted out. Laura released her breath with a whoosh of relief. Harmless Minnie was the mysterious prowler. When the Newfoundland saw the women, she gave a happy bark and galloped toward them, heedless of the flowers underfoot.

"Where did she come from?" Carol asked. "Not the same path we used."

"I have no idea," Laura said, using the dog's collar to urge her out of the bluebell patch. "But Terry did say there's a whole network of paths. She must have used one we haven't tried yet." She resolved to ask Lord Alan if a more detailed map of the grounds was available. While she loved exploring, it would be all too easy to get lost out here.

Lady Freya glanced up from the desk when they straggled into the lobby a while later, having gotten lost as Laura feared. Instead of guiding them back to the castle, Minnie had tromped off without them, drawn by something in the woods.

"Hot tea?" the hostess asked. "With biscuits?" She smiled, her eyes twinkling. "Or I suppose I should say cookies."

"Whatever you call them, I'm sure they're delicious," Carol said.

"It'll be good to sit for a minute," Laura added. "We're trying to decide what to do next."

Their hostess lowered her voice to a whisper. "How about searching Charlotte's room before I clean? The police have released it."

Laura's heart rate ticked up a notch in spite of her weary limbs. "We definitely should do that." She glanced up the staircase. What if someone else got there first? Maybe they should wait to have their snack. "Is the room locked?"

Lady Freya patted her pocket. "I have the key right here. You ladies have a seat and I'll be right back with a tray."

Carol and Molly shared a sofa while Laura took an armchair. She lifted her feet to a hassock. "Ah, this is so comfortable." To think she'd believed this trip would be relaxing. But better to be too busy than bored, right? Not that she could ever be bored at a baking workshop in Scotland.

"Here we are." Lady Freya reappeared with the promised tray. She set it on a low table, then sat to pour and hand around cups of tea. A plate of assorted biscuits also made the rounds.

"How many times a day do you drink tea?" Laura asked out of curiosity. She certainly didn't drink coffee as often. If she did, she'd be awake all night.

"As many as required," Lady Freya said. She lifted a cup to her lips, holding the saucer underneath. "Any and all occasions call for tea."

"How is Lord Alan?" Carol asked. "I haven't seen him lately."

Lady Freya nodded toward the closed office door. "He's holed up with a project. I don't mind, really. I think it's keeping his mind off things."

"Do you have a detailed map of the grounds?" Laura asked. "We got a little turned around this afternoon." Although they could see the castle frequently through the woods, the paths wound around in such a way that they'd had to retrace their steps several times.

"We do," Lady Freya said. "It's not completely accurate since it's very, very old. We're updating it as we restore the gardens. Terry—" She broke off. After a moment, she went on. "Terry grew up exploring these gardens so he's been indispensable. God willing, he will be cleared and return to us soon."

"Did they arrest him?" Laura asked, knowing there were often procedural steps between being taken in and an actual arrest.

Lady Freya's hands shook as she set down her teacup. "Yes, I'm afraid so. The next step is a hearing to see if he will be released on bail. We'll pay it, of course."

"He's fortunate to have you in his corner," Molly said. "Hopefully the case will never go to trial."

"I'm praying he will be cleared well before it does," Lady Freya said. She glanced around at their cups and the decimated plate of biscuits. "Are you ready to go up?"

Charlotte's room was at the other end of the massive upstairs hall from where the ladies were staying. She had occupied a lovely suite overlooking the loch, the wallpaper and draperies done in a lovely shade of blue shot with silver threads. "This is one of our finest rooms," Lady Freya said with a note of pride. "Many members of the royal family have stayed here throughout the centuries."

That the police had searched the room was evident, judging by the drawers and wardrobe doors standing open. Even the bedcovers had been flung back so they could reach under the mattress for anything hidden there. Items from a trash can lay scattered on the floor.

Lady Freya clucked in annoyance as she moved toward the bed. "I suppose I'd better strip this all the way. The sheets need to be changed anyway."

"We can do it, Lady Freya," Laura said. "After we finish looking around." It would be far easier to poke around without being watched.

Laura already felt uncomfortable, as if she were invading Charlotte's privacy. But the snooping was for a good cause, she reminded herself.

"All right, if you insist." Lady Freya pointed to a spot by the door. "Just put the sheets and towels in a heap, and Mrs. Beasley will come get them later."

"Does Mrs. Beasley stay at the castle?" Laura asked. Maybe the cook had noticed something relevant to the case. In her experience, especially a long-ago stint as a personal chef, people often didn't pay attention to domestic help, speaking freely in front of them as if they didn't have ears.

"No, she lives in the village and comes in every day," Lady Freya said. "Besides cooking, she helps with light cleaning and laundry. We have other helpers come in for the heavy work and caterers do our events, like the reception you attended."

"We'll get to work, Lady Freya," Laura said, thinking she still wanted to question Mrs. Beasley. "And we'll let you know right away if we find anything helpful."

"Thank you. I'll be down at the desk if you need me." Her hand on the brass doorknob, Lady Freya added, "By the way, the garden party is still happening tomorrow afternoon. Lord Sebastian said he hopes you three will attend." She slipped out and the door shut gently behind her.

"Is it just me, or did that sound ominous?" Carol asked.

Molly patted her friend on the back. "At this point, everything is ominous. We were spooked by a dog, for goodness' sake."

Laura looked around the suite, doing her best to remain objective as she pushed down a squeamish sensation. "All right. We have the bathroom, the closet, and the room in general to search. Who wants to go where?"

Molly went into the bathroom while Carol offered to go through the closet, including Charlotte's pockets. Laura took the rest of the room, searching under the bed, through the bureau, and anywhere else she could think to look.

If Charlotte had a laptop or tablet, it was gone, hopefully taken by the police for analysis. There was nothing else in the desk area except balls of crumpled paper and the upended trash can. She picked up the rubbish, glancing at each item: a ripped baggage claim tag, granola bar wrappers, and an empty bottle of water. Not much there, but of course the room had been cleaned every day. Laura straightened out one of the crumpled balls. *DAY: CASTLE TOWER*, read one header. Laura recognized the format as that of a screenplay.

She checked the other pieces of paper. They all appeared to be from the same work. There was a main character named Alaina, and another named Lord MacArthur. It seemed Charlotte had been inspired by the surroundings to write her own dramatic work. But where was the rest of the draft? Had the police taken it?

Laura pulled open the desk drawers. In the bottom drawer, under a directory to the area, she found a lined notebook. Glancing through, she saw scrawled notes that were roughly written scenes between Alaina and Lord MacArthur.

Carol stepped out of the closet, her hand outstretched. "Not much here but this."

Molly emerged from the bathroom at the same moment. "Well, that was a bust. Nothing but high-end skin products and makeup." She noticed the card in Carol's fingers. "What do you have there?"

"Agnes's card, which Charlotte probably picked up downstairs." Carol handed Molly the business card.

Molly scanned the card, then walked across the carpet and gave it to Laura. *Agnes McVie, Scottish Heritage Baked Goods* was emblazoned across the top, and it was adorned with a logo of a thistle and a loaf of bread.

That's weird. Laura shook her head. "This isn't a recent card. She has her initials as a logo now, probably because she's so much more well-known." She set the card on the desk and searched on her phone. "This is her current website."

Molly frowned as she examined the imagery. "So what does this old card mean? Probably nothing, right?"

Someone tapped on the door, then twisted the knob. Instinctively, Laura grabbed the card and held it behind her back, then relaxed when she saw it was Lady Freya. Their hostess slipped into the room and shut the door.

"How are you making out?" Lady Freya asked. "I couldn't resist coming up to check in."

"We haven't found much," Laura admitted. "An old business card and pages from a screenplay."

Lady Freya's eyes widened in recognition. "Oh, Charlotte's screenplay. I forgot about that. Alan is reading the draft. She asked him to check it for historical accuracy and give his opinion."

A full draft did exist, then. Acting more from instinct rather than certainty that the screenplay related to Charlotte's death, Laura asked, "Can we take a look at it?"

"Of course," Lady Freya said. "Alan will be more than happy to let you read it."

After helping to strip the beds and gather the towels as they had offered, the women went downstairs to talk to Lord Alan. Laura kept the business card as a possible clue, and the notebook, planning to study it in more depth. She also brought along the screenplay pages to show the laird, who was holed up in his office.

Lady Freya opened the office door and peeked in. "Is this a good time to interrupt you, dear?" Her husband grumbled something back and she pushed the door wide. "Go on in, ladies." The telephone rang at the front desk. "I'd better get that." She scurried off.

Lord Alan was seated behind his desk, the pages of a book manuscript in front of him. He took off a pair of glasses and smiled. "How can I help you?" He patted the pile. "I'm just proofreading my latest book."

"Sorry to interrupt." Laura placed the still rumpled screenplay pages on the desk. "We found these in Charlotte's room. Lady Freya said you have a copy of Charlotte's screenplay."

With a nod, Lord Alan tugged open a desk drawer. He pulled out another sheaf of papers, this one much slimmer than his book. "She gave it to me to read. Quite good, actually, for a first attempt. Both in general and for this subject."

"What's it about?" Carol asked.

"Please, have a seat," Lord Alan offered with a wave. There were two visitor chairs close to the desk, and Laura pulled up a third from a corner. "The short answer is, an heiress comes to Scotland seeking to claim her property. Quite exciting really."

"Is it set in the past?" Molly asked.

"No, present day," Lord Alan said. "But it does have a historical component." He sat back and swiveled his chair gently. "The heiress is on the trail of Jacobite gold."

"Jacobite gold?" Laura remembered that Lord Alan was interested in that topic. "Did she want your expertise regarding that?"

He played with a pen, rolling it between his fingers. "That was one aspect she wanted my feedback on. And the writing flow, setting, and so forth."

"Of course," Molly said. "She must have been excited to work with a renowned author such as yourself."

A small smile on Lord Alan's face revealed that the flattery had hit its mark. "Well, I wouldn't say renowned, but well-regarded in the canon of Scottish works? Perhaps."

Laura allowed the man his moment in the sun but was eager to dig a little deeper. "How likely is it that gold was left here?" She had always had a hard time imagining that people or pirates, in other lore, would go off and leave such valuables behind.

"It is a long and involved tale," Lord Alan said. "Do you have the time? I'll try to keep it brief." Despite the disclaimers, his eyes gleamed with excitement.

Laura guessed he was quite eager to discuss a favorite topic. "We have time," she said. It was probably a long shot that this had anything to do with Charlotte's death, but either way, she still found the topic interesting.

Lord Alan sketched out the general history first, how the Scottish clans had regarded Charles Edward Stuart, or Bonnie Prince Charlie, as the true king of England. The grandson of James II, Charlie had been raised in Italy. In 1745, Charlie landed on Scotland's shores, intending to carry out a rebellion that would place his family back on the throne. But it all failed, resulting in the destruction of the clans and the exile of many Scottish men, women, and children to America.

"The Battle of Culloden," Carol murmured. "Scotland's Waterloo."

Lord Alan bestowed an approving nod. "That's exactly right. Now, as to the gold. French allies brought chests of gold and other supplies from France and Spain to support the cause after Culloden. In the unstable situation, the gold was moved and hidden many times. Part of it was never recovered, leading to charges of embezzlement." He paused. "But some of us have reason to believe a significant chunk was hidden here, on the shores of Loch Glenellen."

"You found documents stating that, you mean?" Laura asked, curious as to what led to that conclusion.

Lord Alan swiveled his chair again. "Exactly. I have discovered several references to the gold in family papers, just enough to tantalize.

Including mention of a supposed deathbed confession from a man who handled the gold." He chuckled. "No map marked with an X, of course. But this area had many Jacobite supporters, and there are lots of secret routes used by smugglers long ago. Combine all that, and it's hard not to believe the gold could easily be on this land somewhere."

"And Charlotte wrote about it in her screenplay," Laura said, impressed with the actress's clever plotting. A treasure hunt was a great premise for a movie, especially if based on real events.

"Yes, and she picked my brain quite thoroughly. Hopefully she didn't ask around anywhere else. Who knows what sort of inaccuracies she might have picked up from the amateur enthusiasts around here?" Lord Alan chuckled and put his hand to his lapel. "No need to ask elsewhere. I got high honors in history from Cambridge."

Laura recalled seeing Charlotte visiting Glenellen Manor earlier that week. "Is it possible that Charlotte asked Lord Sebastian about the gold? We saw her go into the manor a few days ago."

"Really?" Lord Alan's brows rose. "She didn't mention she was consulting with the old fellow, though he does have quite an interest in the topic. I hope he didn't feed her too much misleading information. That abounds, as I'm sure you can guess. I myself am meticulous in my research."

Laura didn't doubt it, but she was more focused on discovering the reason for Charlotte's visit to the manor. And why had MacVail treated the actress so distantly at the reception? One would think they would greet each other like acquaintances, if not friends. Had they argued, with Charlotte perhaps challenging his knowledge? Or was there more to the encounter than met the eye?

While Laura pondered, Molly changed the subject. "I'm looking forward to the garden party. I understand the manor is worth visiting."

"Oh, it's historic, all right," Lord Alan said. "Built by a lesser son of this house in the mid-1700s. Lord Sebastian is descended from that branch." He glanced down at his pile of pages.

The women exchanged glances, then took the hint and rose.

"Thanks for your help, Lord Alan," Laura said brightly. "One more thing. Do you mind if we read Charlotte's screenplay? I have to admit being curious." She didn't mention their investigation, since she wasn't sure if Lady Freya had told him.

"I don't mind a bit." He handed her the sheaf of papers. "But please be careful with it, and don't take it out of the castle. I'm not sure what will happen to it now. But it's too good to be forgotten about, I know that much."

Laura clutched the screenplay to her chest. Besides offering a good read, she hoped that the screenplay might provide clues to Charlotte's death. Otherwise they didn't have much to go on so far.

Not for the first time, Laura was daunted by the enormity of their quest. If they failed, an innocent man could go to jail.

B y mutual consent, the friends retreated to their rooms for the rest of the afternoon. Molly planned to scour the tabloids for clues, while Carol wanted to catch up with Harvey and relax. As for Laura, she decided to read the screenplay.

But she was only a page in when her phone rang. When she saw who was calling, she grinned. "Hey, big brother."

"I prefer older brother," Brody drawled.

"Older doesn't mean wiser."

"Touché. How's Scotland?" he asked.

"Do you want the short version or the long version?"

He chuckled, and Laura could hear the squeak of his desk chair as he leaned back. He must be at his law office, where he handled wills and trusts. "My next client meeting isn't for an hour. I have time."

"Well, buckle up," Laura warned. "A television show is filming here, and guess what? The lead actress was murdered."

A stunned silence followed, and Laura could imagine her brother's face. "I'm not sure what I was expecting you to say, but it definitely wasn't that." His tone sharpened. "Are you talking about Charlotte Martin, from that *Highland Lass* show? It's been all over the news today. I didn't make the connection until now."

Laura wasn't surprised. In this digital age, news traveled across the globe with the click of a button. "The very same. And I was the one who found her."

"Yikes, sis. That's terrible."

"Not as terrible for me as for poor Charlotte," Laura said sadly, then told him about that fateful morning jog and Terry's subsequent arrest. "Lady Freya asked us to investigate. She got wind somehow that we solved Douglas Kinnaird's murder."

"Seriously?" Brody grunted in amazement. "I thought you went there to bake bread, not to become international crime fighters."

"Maybe we have a knack for solving mysteries," Laura said, feeling a rush of pride at the notion that she and her friends could discover hidden talents even though they were in their fifties.

"Well you certainly have a knack for finding mysteries, at least," Brody said. "You found the body, after all."

Laura shrugged, even though her brother couldn't see her. "It was an accident. Anyone who came along would have seen her." If it hadn't been her, then Lord Sebastian would have discovered Charlotte. *Unless he put her there.* She felt a chill. Was he a killer returning to the scene of the crime?

"So I assume you agreed to her ladyship's request," Brody said.

"We didn't have the heart to say no," Laura replied. "Lady Freya is a darling, and she doesn't deserve this negative publicity. I have the feeling they need to run the castle as an inn or else they will lose it."

Brody tapped on some keys. "I'm looking at their website now. It's a gorgeous place. But yeah, the maintenance costs must be staggering."

"So you can see why we have to try. The film crew was supposed to return for another season, but that could be out the window now. All she has is her reputation with guests like us. And this place is spectacular."

"I can see that. And so historic." He whistled, apparently still exploring the website. "Built when? Wow."

"Speaking of history, get this: Lord Alan—Lady Freya's husband—believes Jacobite gold is buried here somewhere."

Brody groaned. "Now I'm envious. How cool is that? If you stumble across the treasure hoard, don't forget your dear older brother."

"Ha! Don't expect a cut," Laura said. "Lord and Lady Cameron will probably need every penny to keep this place." Her room phone rang. "Sorry, I've got to go."

"Don't do anything I wouldn't do," Brody warned, then disconnected the call.

Rolling her eyes, Laura answered the room phone. "Hello?"

"It's Carol. Lady Freya offered to send up dinner in a while. Want to eat in my room? We can go over the case."

"Sounds good to me," Laura said, and they set a time. Then she picked up page two of the screenplay.

Mrs. Beasley delivered the evening meal on a rolling cart. "Did you climb the stairs with that?" Laura asked as she let the woman into Carol's room.

"There's a service elevator," the cook said. "Used only by the staff." The taciturn cook took her time laying out the dishes on the table near the window. She had brought individual potpies and a large bowl of salad to share.

"Good thing," Carol said. "This place is huge."

Molly rapped on the door and walked in, holding a large notepad. "You won't believe—" She stopped short, seeing that they weren't alone. "Hi, Mrs. Beasley. Dinner sure smells good."

Mrs. Beasley merely nodded in acknowledgment of the compliment. She placed rolled napkins holding silverware at each place. "When you're done, load the dishes on the cart and put it in the hall. Someone will come get it."

Laura's brain whirred with possible questions for the cook since this was a great opportunity to question her. Before she could formulate something, Carol asked, "Are you from Glenellen, Mrs. Beasley? It's a beautiful village."

"I was born and raised here. Lived in Edinburgh for a while, but after Mr. Beasley died, I moved back." She pressed her thin lips together as though regretting the remark had escaped.

Laura saw an opening. "Did you go to school with Terry?" She guessed the cook and the gardener were about the same age, in Lady Freya's generation.

Mrs. Beasley picked up a pitcher of water, the cubes clinking as she placed it on the table. "He was in my class. Always was a bit off, if you know what I mean."

"Really?" Laura asked, unable to hide her confusion. Did she mean violent? Or introverted? Perhaps Terry had learning disabilities.

"Put it this way, I'm not surprised." The cook pointed to an electric kettle on a sideboard. "You can boil water in that for tea. I've brought you mugs." She glanced around the table then wiped her hands on her apron. "Enjoy."

The women took seats at the table. Carol unrolled her silverware and settled her napkin on her lap. "That was a terrible thing to say about Terry."

Laura followed suit with her own napkin. "Totally. Casting aspersions, they call it. She didn't come right out and say it, but she obviously thinks Terry is guilty."

"She's the only one, then." Molly filled three glasses with ice water. "Well, except the police." She handed the glasses around.

Laura picked up her fork and pierced the potpie crust, releasing fragrant steam. The first bite was perfect—a blend of chicken, potato, carrots, and peas in thick gravy, cradled by a flaky, buttery crust. Mrs.

Beasley was a talented cook, she had to give her that. "This is so good," she said. "Why don't we shelve our discussion until after we eat?"

"I agree with that," Carol said. "The whole thing ties me up in knots."

A short while later, every bit of potpie was gone and very little remained of the salad. The women cleaned up, then settled in the sitting area with cups of tea. Carol switched on the gas fireplace, and the leaping flames provided a sense of cozy comfort.

"This is so nice," Molly said. She pulled out her phone and snapped a picture of Laura and Carol sitting side by side on the sofa, mugs in hand. "Something to remember this trip by."

Carol put up a hand. "As long as you don't go posting it online. My hair is a mess and my makeup is long gone."

"I won't," Molly promised. "But I will send it to Harvey in response to the pic he just texted me of him and Angus lounging on the couch." She brought up the image and showed it around.

"You're going to have a hard time prying those two apart," Laura said with a laugh.

"Don't I know it?" Molly agreed, then she put away her phone and grabbed her notepad. She leafed through the pages. "All right. I did my research online. Would you like to hear what I found out?"

"Yes please," Laura said. She leaned back in the armchair and rested her feet on a hassock.

Molly cleared her throat. "Okay. I did confirm that Charlotte and Finn dated for almost a year. They met when Finn was finishing up a supporting stage role in Edinburgh. Charlotte had made some appearances on a British sitcom, but nothing huge. So, *A Highland Lass* was a big break for both of them."

"I can see that," Carol said. "Star roles on a long-running show is the brass ring, right? Besides a part in a blockbuster movie, I mean."

"The big money is in movies," Molly said. "But television work is steady, and in some rare cases, even better than movies. I've heard of stars getting a million dollars per episode before."

"Wow." Laura tried to imagine having a paycheck that size. "Are we in the wrong business or what?"

The others laughed. "It's almost like winning the lottery," Molly said. "Though of course they work really, really hard to get anywhere."

"And that might anger someone who thinks Charlotte is hurting their career," Carol mused. "I can understand. The motivation, I mean, not the murder."

Laura put herself in the place of the other actors in the show. How disheartening to achieve a foothold only to have it all collapse—and not only for the actors. "The production team must not be happy either," she said. "What about Clive? Isn't his career at risk too? If the network cancels the show, it would be a major setback for him."

Molly nodded at Laura. "Bingo. Clive created this show and got the network interested. He's both producer and director." She leaned forward, her eyes bright in the firelight. "And he had violent incidents in his past."

"No." Carol's mouth hung open in amazement. "Did you learn any details?"

"Did I ever." Molly shuffled through the notepad. "Listen to this." She read aloud an account of Clive losing his temper with a camera operator that he claimed had spoiled an important shot for an earlier show he'd directed. Despite resorting to physical violence, Clive had merely gotten his wrist slapped by the court. The camera operator had been fired.

A cold sensation nestled in Laura's stomach. "If he found out Charlotte was quitting," she said slowly, "and saw his show going up in smoke . . ."

"That's what I thought," Molly said, nodding solemnly along with Carol. "Although it's really counterproductive to kill your star. Why not negotiate, offer more money or something?"

"Maybe he didn't have that much power," Carol suggested. "And if Charlotte didn't want to work with him anymore, he wouldn't want her to say that to the executives holding the purse strings."

Laura sipped her tea, thinking this all over. Much of it was guesswork, but she felt it was a solid lead. Clive had a temper, Charlotte had wanted to leave, and that would anger the director. And now Charlotte was dead.

"All right," Molly said. "In the interests of being objective, on to the next suspect. Finn." She sighed.

"I thought we decided he probably didn't do it," Laura said.

"His grief and shock certainly appear real." Molly sipped her tea with a pensive air. "Then again, he's an actor, and a fine one at that. So we need to take a second look, just in case."

"More tea?" At nods from her friends, Carol rose from the sofa and switched on the electric kettle. "What do we know about Finn? Not only was this his first starring role, but he and Charlotte were involved. And she broke up with him."

"That's correct, Carol." Molly flipped through a stack of printouts tucked into the notepad. "I found a lot of news items about their romance. Pictures of them out in public, a story about love on the set, and so on."

"I want to read the one about love on the set." Laura reached out her hand, and Molly passed it over.

The article was short, only a few paragraphs of text describing how thrilled the pair was to work together, and how perfect each thought the other was for the role. Two pictures illustrated the story. One showed them sitting close together at an outside café in Edinburgh.

The other was from the set, a conversation between the stars while other members of the crew watched.

"Check out Kyla's face," Laura said, handing the article back. "She looks really angry." In fact, she was glaring at the couple, who were standing close together, Charlotte's hands on Finn's shoulders.

Molly took another peek. "Oh, I see what you mean. She's not in the scene, so she wasn't acting." She gave the paper to Carol. "That's how she really felt."

"She wasn't happy about her brother dating Charlotte," Laura concluded. "I wonder how deep her dislike went."

"You never know." The kettle boiled and Carol flipped off the switch. "The combination of Charlotte breaking Finn's heart and leaving the show might have pushed Kyla over the edge."

Laura took a moment to imagine the scene. But she could easily replace Kyla with Clive or even Finn. There was nothing concrete to eliminate any of their suspects. Yet.

Carol gathered their mugs and made fresh cups of tea. "I think we've done good work tonight, ladies," she said. "Why don't we take a break and talk about something a little more fun?"

"What's that?" Molly organized her papers in a neat stack.

"What we are going to wear to the garden party tomorrow." Carol handed around the tea. "I noticed there was a dress shop in the village, Sally Forth. Who wants to go shopping?"

"Me!" Molly volunteered, then picked up her phone and scrolled through. "Judging by these other garden parties, we need a pretty dress and a hat."

"A hat?" Laura was aghast. She only wore hats in winter, when she had to or her ears would freeze off.

"A hat," Molly repeated. "Preferably with flowers and ribbons on it to match the pretty dress you're going to buy."

Carol settled back onto the sofa. "Oh my. This should be interesting."

"Take the car to the village or walk?" Molly asked Laura and Carol after breakfast the next morning. "I'm fine either way."

Laura glanced out the dining room window, seeing another beautiful day. "I think we should walk. This is the trip of a lifetime, right?"

Carol set down her coffee cup. "True. And after yet another full Scottish breakfast, I can use the exercise." Her deep, rich laugh rang out, earning a smile from Lady Freya, who was clearing the buffet table.

"Are you going down to the village?" Lady Freya asked. "If you go soon, you should have time before the baking lesson after lunch. It's a short session today due to the garden party." Using mitts, she picked up a warming tray and placed it on the cart.

"That's why we're going down," Molly said. "We decided we need new outfits for the occasion."

"Sally Forth is good." Lady Freya pulled the cart along the table to the next empty pan. "If you mention my name, the owner will give you a discount."

Molly grinned at her friends. "Good to know. Thanks."

The trio agreed to meet in the lobby ten minutes later, then they went upstairs to get ready for the excursion. Laura filled a water bottle and grabbed some packaged biscuits for a snack, chuckling to herself at the fact that, after another hearty breakfast, there was no way she'd be hungry anytime soon.

Laura arrived in the lobby first and saw Lord Alan seated in his office with the door open. She rapped on the doorframe. "Sorry to interrupt, but I have a question for you."

Lord Alan rose from his seat. "Of course, Laura. Come in. How can I help you?"

"We're walking down to the village again today, and that made me think of something. Lady Freya mentioned that a detailed map of the garden exists. Do you have a copy? Terry had referred to a network of paths, but the tourist map doesn't show them."

Lord Alan stroked his chin. "That's because we don't want people stumbling around out there and getting lost. There are cellar holes where buildings once stood, that kind of thing."

"We'll be careful." Laura thought a map might assist with the investigation. How exactly, she wasn't sure. But better knowledge of the property might help them figure out what happened the night of Charlotte's death, with people coming and going.

"I've got something somewhere..." Lord Alan went to a bookcase and began flipping through stacks of documents. "Tell you what, I'll find it and make a copy. Come see me later."

"That would be fantastic." Laura heard Molly and Carol chatting as they descended the stairs, so she said goodbye to the laird and hurried to join them.

Since they had limited time, the women took the path through the woods. The way was becoming familiar to Laura now and it seemed that they reached the loch path in no time at all.

Laura enjoyed gazing out at the water and the mountains beyond. Every day, the hillsides appeared lusher and greener as summer advanced. Sweeps of yellow revealed where gorse bushes grew. But as they approached the height of land from where she'd seen Charlotte in the water, her midsection tightened. Maybe coming this way wasn't such a good idea.

She was watching her feet, ostensibly to make sure she didn't trip on anything, but really it was to avoid looking at the spot where she'd stumbled upon a murder. So when Carol grabbed her arm, Laura nearly jumped out of her skin. "What's he doing?" Carol whispered.

Laura glanced up to see a man standing on the edge of the cliff taking photographs. He wore a navy-blue windbreaker, jeans, and sneakers, his unruly hair ruffled by the breeze. With a hard expression on his face, he didn't look like a tourist. Then it sank in. "I bet he's from the press."

They heard steady footsteps approaching and spun around together to find the source. Finn Paterson bore down on them, dressed in running shorts, T-shirt, and sneakers. But then he caught sight of the photographer, and his face darkened with rage.

"What do you think you're doing?" Finn shouted. He sped up and tore past the women, leaving the path to approach the other man.

The reporter glanced at Finn. "What's it look like, mate? Doing my job." He started to turn back around, lifting his camera to his eye.

To Laura's stunned disbelief, Finn wrested the camera from the reporter and threw it onto the ground. He stomped on it a couple of times, then tossed it off the cliff. The women gasped as the camera made a wide arc through the air, landing in deep water with a splash.

"What'd you do that for?" The reporter gaped at the drop-off. Then he became angry. "That was a brand-new camera. You owe me big time, mate."

Finn began running again. "The name is Finn Paterson. Send me a bill at the castle." He pivoted and jogged backward for a moment. "And no more pictures at this spot. Or else."

"Or else what?" the reporter grumbled. Seeing the women staring at him, he hollered, "What are you looking at?" Shoving his hands into his windbreaker pockets, he trudged toward the village. A short distance down the path, he pulled out a phone and began squawking his displeasure to whoever was on the other end.

The women stared at each other in shock. Laura could understand Finn's dismay at coming across someone trying to profit from Charlotte's death. But to actually destroy valuable property? That was way over the top.

"I can't believe Finn did such a thing," Molly said, her face solemn. "I guess he's prone to outbursts too." The implications of her remark fell over them like a shadow.

If the handsome actor had no qualms about angrily tossing an expensive camera over the cliff in front of witnesses, what was he capable of doing when nobody was watching?

They continued on along the path, each lost in her own thoughts. As they passed the manor house, Laura saw vans pulling up the drive and the peaks of a white tent in the side yard. Classical music drifted from the house, where doors and windows stood open. Seeing the party preparations underway, a burst of anticipation lifted Laura's spirits. She, ordinary Laura Donovan, was attending a garden party in company with Scottish lords and ladies.

"I can't wait until this afternoon," Molly said, echoing Laura's thoughts. "I feel like I'm living in a storybook."

"We're going to be really spoiled after this trip," Carol said with a snort of laughter. "Our friends and family won't know what to do with us."

"Shall I start now?" Molly joked. She curtsied and gestured to the path. "After you, milady." She then curtsied toward Laura. "And you as well, milady."

Laura pictured people calling her by a title all the time and had to chuckle at the idea. Maybe it was easier if one grew up with it, like Lord Alan and Lady Freya.

Cheered by the banter, the women covered the remaining distance to the village at a good clip. "Where is the dress shop?" Laura asked Molly. "I don't remember seeing it last time we came."

"It's on a side street that intersects the main street." Molly glanced at the signs marking the lanes running up the hill from the harbor. "Ah, here we go. Thistle Lane."

The dress shop was in a whitewashed structure a couple of buildings up from the corner. An adjacent storefront's bay window displayed an array of footwear, from leather boots and lace-up shoes to sandals, mules, and pumps.

"Do we need shoes?" Carol asked hopefully.

"Maybe," Molly said. "I guess it will depend on what dresses we buy."

Laura had only packed black heels, boots, and running shoes, so she'd likely need to stop at the shoe shop after choosing a dress.

The air inside Sally Forth was warm and lightly perfumed, the lighting was soft, and the walls painted a pale pink. Uncrowded display racks showcased beautiful dresses, and along one wall was a row of mannequin heads holding a variety of hats. Laura felt more feminine just stepping inside.

An older woman with high-piled gray hair stepped from behind a counter when they entered. "How may I help you?" she asked in a charming Scottish accent. "I'm Sally, at your service."

Molly took the lead and introduced them. "We're attending Lord Sebastian's garden party this afternoon and we need dresses. And hats."

Sally clasped her hands together. "Oh, what a treat it is to attend one of Lord Sebastian's parties. It will be an honor to dress you for the occasion."

Laura glanced at Carol, who was barely suppressing a grin. Once again Laura felt as if she had stepped between the pages of a book. Sally was treating them like royalty.

"We'll be depending on your recommendations," Molly said. "We've never attended such an event."

The shopkeeper looked them over, asked a couple of questions, then flipped through the racks of dresses. One by one, she ushered them into a fitting room with three or four dresses to try on.

Laura looked over her three selections, all knee-length dresses in hues that flattered Laura's coloring. One was a traditional large-scale floral, one was a solid-hued crepe, and one was a pale green wrap dress with a tiny ivory leaf design that Laura pegged as her favorite. Sally knew her business.

"What do you think?" Carol asked a few minutes later. Laura peeked around the curtain to see her friend posing in front of a three-way mirror. The coral sheath with a flattering fit made Carol's dark skin glow.

"I love it," Laura said.

"Me too," Molly agreed from the other dressing room. "Here I come." She pushed her curtain aside and stepped through, revealing a silk dress that hit at the knee. The subtle cream, pink, and pale blue floral print complemented her petite body.

Carol cocked her head and studied her friend. "Very nice. It looks great with your hair."

Molly fluffed her blonde locks. "You think so?" She twirled around with a laugh. "I feel so pretty."

"Your turn, Laura," Carol said. "You can't hide forever."

Having tried on the other two dresses, Laura slipped into the one she liked best. She smoothed the skirt and peered into the mirror, pleased with what she saw—and even more pleased with how comfortable she felt. "Okay, I'm coming."

Molly clapped appreciatively when Laura emerged. "You're gorgeous!"

"Now that's a dress," Carol said approvingly.

Channeling her inner supermodel, Laura strode toward the three-way mirror and pivoted dramatically, eliciting giggles and more applause from her friends.

"Very nice, ladies," Sally said. "You'll be the belles of the garden party. Wait here and I'll select hats."

"I feel like we're in a movie," Molly murmured as they waited for Sally to come back.

Sally returned with two hats and set them on a nearby counter. "Hats can be tricky. Not only do they have to go with your outfit, but they have to suit your features and your overall build." She pointed at Molly. "You, for instance. You are such a lovely wee thing that a large hat would look ridiculous. This, on the other hand, should be just right." She picked up a straw cloche adorned with a cluster of flowers and nestled it onto Molly's head, then put a hand on her back, urging her to turn around. "Take a look."

The hat looked wonderful with her outfit—and as Sally said, was in proportion with Molly's face and form. Molly touched the brim, her eyes sparkling as she gazed into the mirror. "I love it."

Sally smiled and picked up the other hat, a confection of froth and feathers that looked amazing on Carol. The shopkeeper returned to the millinery area for Laura's, an ivory picture hat mad of straw and trimmed with wide ribbon. Despite her usual aversion to ornamental headwear, Laura couldn't help but be charmed by the overall effect it created.

"I hate to take this off," Carol said. "But I suppose we should since we're walking back."

"Where are you staying?" Sally asked.

"At the castle," Molly answered. "Lady Freya sent us."

Sally nodded. "She's so good to me. I'll be taking off ten percent today." She circled a finger. "On everything."

They all thanked her before popping back into the dressing rooms to change. After making the purchases, they went next door into the shoe shop, where Laura bought T-strap pumps, Molly picked out a pair of strappy sandals, and Carol chose classic open-toe heels.

"Want a cup of tea before we head back?" Carol suggested outside the shoe store. "I'm kind of parched."

"How about The Library Tearoom again?" Laura suggested. "I have a question for Una."

The trio strolled down the street carrying their bags. Outside the small grocery, metal racks held stacks of newspapers, almost every headline mentioning Charlotte. Laura wasn't surprised, just saddened. In the fast-paced media world, another story would soon displace that one, but here in Glenellen, the effects would linger.

Una's somber face only underlined that. "Good morning, ladies," she said, rising from her usual chair. "Here for tea?"

"Please," Laura said. She lifted her bags slightly. "We shopped until we dropped."

"Oh, for the garden party?" Una placed menus on a table in the corner. "At first I was surprised Lord Sebastian decided to go on with it, but maybe the village needs something to distract us right now."

"That's what we thought too." Laura set her packages on the ground near the table, then took a seat. "Una, the first time we were here, you said a redheaded woman from the castle was asking about her family." Laura had no idea if this was related to the murder, but any lead was worth pursuing.

"We had two, actually." Una's expression grew even more melancholy. "But one of them was that Charlotte Martin. When I saw the newspaper stories, I recognized her."

So Charlotte thought she had family from the area. That might shine a different light on her screenplay, revealing a more personal interest. Had Charlotte based the main character, an heiress, on herself? Laura hastily dismissed this wild thought.

"Excuse me a moment." Una bustled across the room to the library area. She selected a faded red book from one of the shelves. "She was supposed to borrow this but never came back."

The spine read *Burke's Peerage* in faded gold lettering. An emblem featuring a shield and crown was on the cover. Laura opened the book to discover an alphabetical genealogy, starting with the present holder of a title and followed with a chronological history. She passed it around the table to the others. "Are Scottish titles included?"

Una nodded. "Lord Alan's cousin is mentioned in that edition, which was printed before Lord Alan inherited the title."

"Can women inherit?" Molly asked. "I read once they couldn't."

"In some cases, yes, but many titles pass to male heirs only," Una said. "It can be rather complicated."

Laura indicated the book. "Do you mind if we borrow this?"

"That's what it's here for." Una pointed out a card in the back that Laura could sign and date. "Now what can I get you?"

With a glance at the others, Carol ordered for them. "I think just hot tea all around. Glasses of water too, please. Then we've got to get back to the castle for lunch."

"Coming right up." Una swept away to prepare their drinks.

Molly slouched back in her chair with a sigh. "I'm glad we're taking a break. It's going to be a busy day." She grinned. "And a very exciting one."

A van was parked in front of the castle when they returned, and the lobby was a mass of middle-aged women and piles of luggage.

Lady Freya was behind the desk checking everyone in. "Lunch is in the dining room," she called to Laura and her friends.

"We should take our bags up first," Carol said. "And freshen up. Meet down here in ten?"

As the Bakehouse Three made their way through the new guests,

Laura saw there weren't as many as it seemed—only eight. But they were a lively bunch.

One woman pulled Laura aside near the stairs. "Were you here when Charlotte Martin was killed?" She had a thick Scottish accent, glasses on a chain, and red hair streaked with gray piled in a messy bun.

"I was," Laura said. "But I don't like to talk about it." *Might as well make that plain from the start.*

The woman reared back, putting on her glasses for a better look. "Oh, you're American. We're from the Glasgow Knitting Club. Finally here, after a bout of stomach flu went through us like a bowling ball through ninepins."

Hopefully not still contagious. Laura edged away slightly, though she didn't want to come off as rude. They'd be in Agnes's workshop together, after all. "My friends and I are from Michigan. We own a Scottish bakehouse there."

"Very nice," the woman said. "Well, I'll let you go. Almost time to put on the feed bag." She gave a hearty peal of laughter and turned away, rejoining the line checking in.

As Laura had guessed, the eight new arrivals made for a lively lunch and baking lesson, in which they made lace wafers. Agnes had seemed somewhat frustrated by the boisterous newcomers, who demanded most of the instructor's attention, so Laura had ended up coaching her friends on creating the sweet delicacies. She tried not to think about how little she was actually learning from the famed Agnes McVie. Sure, the course was aimed at amateur chefs, but Laura had thought that she'd at least glean a few helpful tidbits from Agnes.

At four o'clock, Laura and the others drove to the manor. It was only about half a mile away, but they hadn't wanted to walk over in their new shoes.

"Wow. There sure are a lot of people here," Carol said as she crept along the drive crowded with parked cars. They eventually found a spot at the end of the line and got out.

Other guests were strolling along the paved drive toward the manor, the men in summer suits and the women in pretty dresses. Laura was glad they had splurged on new outfits. Anyone looking at the trio would never guess this was their first such occasion, thanks to Sally.

"There's Lady Freya," Molly said, waving. A valet was helping Lady Freya emerge from a vintage black Bentley. Lord Alan handed the valet the keys and held out an elbow to his wife. At Lady Freya's urging, they waited for the three Americans at the base of the stone steps leading up to the manor's front door.

"You look absolutely lovely, my dears." Lady Freya greeted each with a kiss on the cheek and an arm squeeze. "I take it Sally did well by you?"

"She certainly did," Laura said. "Thank you for the recommendation."

As a group, they entered the manor, the door held open by another young man. Laura's gaze swept the entrance hall, taking in polished wood floors, a soaring staircase, and crystal chandeliers. Although tiny compared to the castle, the manor was every bit as magnificent.

"The gardens are this way," Lady Freya said. She led them down a corridor lined with family portraits to the rear, where French doors opened onto a terrace. Food and drink stations were attended by servers in white and black. Clusters of guests milled about the patio and on a lawn bordered by neat flower beds. A string quartet played beneath a small, white tent.

Not knowing anyone, the ladies followed Lady Freya to where Lord Sebastian was standing, greeting his guests. The couple he was talking to moved away and he smiled at them. "So glad you could make it," he said. "It's a beautiful day."

"It certainly is," Laura said. "Thank you for including us. We've wanted to see your home since our first glimpse of it."

He bowed slightly to acknowledge this remark. "I'll give you the nickel tour in a bit, after the rest of my guests arrive."

The ladies stopped at the drinks station for glasses of punch, then circulated around the property. Instead of feeling out of place, Laura decided to enjoy the experience as a spectator. She spotted Kyla, Clive, and Finn, but the television people were surrounded by other guests eager to meet them. Laura and her friends found three lawn chairs set up near the string quartet and sat for a while, people-watching and listening to classical music. Molly discreetly took photographs of the party, including a few of her friends.

"I think it's time for our tour," Carol said, nodding toward Lord Sebastian, who was scanning the crowd from his perch on the terrace. She lifted a hand to let him know they'd seen him.

Once the women met up with the nobleman, he swiftly ushered them into the house. As they entered, Laura realized that she'd been expecting to be greeted by the laird's dog, Mack. "I suppose Mack isn't a fan of garden parties," she joked.

Lord Sebastian chuckled good-naturedly. "Oh, I'm certain he'd love to attend, but he spends most of his time at the farm down the way. I just borrow him for a stroll from time to time." He cleared his throat, then began their tour. "When I inherited the place, it was in quite a state. Fortunately, most of the original features had been preserved."

He showed them the library first, mentioning it had been painted fire-engine red before his time. Now the room, filled with enviable floor-to-ceiling bookcases, was tastefully painted in shades of pale gray.

"I consulted with many experts during the process," he explained. "I wanted the place to be modern and livable while retaining its character and historical integrity." He threw open double doors with a flourish. "This is my favorite room in the house. Feel free to look around."

Laura gazed around at the gracious yet comfortable drawing room with its pale green silk wallpaper, carved white woodwork and columns, and velvet-upholstered furniture. As they explored the space, she spotted a half-open door and peeked inside, discovering a smaller sitting room decorated in a feminine style. From her reading, she knew that ladies often had their own private rooms where they did correspondence and took care of household business.

But what really caught her eye was a portrait of a young woman over the fireplace. Dressed in tartan with long red hair hanging loose, the painting's subject held a book in both hands. The background depicted the manor and the hills beyond, most likely to show she was a former resident of this house. But what struck Laura the most was that she looked almost exactly like Charlotte Martin.

14

A hand reached in front of Laura and gently closed the door. "I'm sorry," Lord Sebastian said. "But that room isn't on the tour."

"I see." Laura itched to ask about the painting, but the laird's stern expression deterred her. She was a guest in his home after all.

As they followed Lord Sebastian through the rest of the house, including an impressive paneled dining room and a conservatory filled with orchids and other exotic plants, Laura's thoughts kept returning to the portrait. Was Charlotte a relative? Was that why she had been visiting Lord Sebastian the day she died?

Was that relationship why she died?

"What's the matter?" Carol whispered to Laura as they walked back onto the terrace. "You look like you're a million miles away."

Laura glanced around. "I can't talk about it here. After we leave."

After fixing Laura with an appraising gaze for a moment, Carol finally nodded. "Okay. Anyway, those strawberries are calling me." She gestured toward the food buffet, where huge bowls of fresh, ripe strawberries had been brought out. Servers were topping each individual dish with a snowy dollop of cream.

"Me too," Molly said, joining the line. "I always love the first strawberries of the summer. And I bet that cream is from a local farm."

According to what they overheard in line, it was indeed local cream, and the strawberries were grown just outside the village. Serving the first berries of the year was an annual tradition, one that the Bakehouse Three reveled in sharing.

As she waited her turn, Laura glanced around and noticed that Agnes had joined the party and was standing nearby. The pastry chef wore a flowing top and skirt of turquoise silk and had her hair up in a French twist.

"You look familiar," a guest said to Agnes. "Are you from around here?"

Agnes laughed, multiple bangle bracelets clashing as she flapped a hand. "Oh no, I'm from Glasgow. This is my first trip to Glenellen." Her smile held a touch of smugness. "But you may have seen my television program, *Baking the Classics with Agnes.*"

The woman she was speaking to shrieked in excitement. "Come to think of it, I have seen that. I love your show."

Agnes turned with narrowed eyes, as if sensing Laura was listening. Laura quickly faced front again, not wanting to get on the instructor's bad side. The line moved forward at a snail's pace, but finally she reached the buffet table and was handed a cut-glass bowl of strawberries and cream.

Although Mack the collie wasn't attending the party, Minnie made an unexpected appearance while Laura and her friends were perched on the terrace wall eating strawberries. The huge dog trotted through the tight-packed crowd, practically knocking people over in her eagerness to reach the Bakehouse Three. In fact, she went right past her mistress in search of her new friends.

Molly laughed and patted Minnie's massive head. "What are you doing here?"

To Laura's surprise, the dog opened her jaws and dropped a muddy strip of cloth at their feet. Through the grime, Laura recognized the red and green Cameron tartan.

"What is that?" Carol asked. "Did she dig it up somewhere?"

"I have no idea." Laura used her napkin to pick up the cloth, thinking she would toss it into the trash. "Dogs," she said to the people standing nearby. Now that Minnie had done her duty, she flopped down on all fours with a groan and began panting.

Molly held out her hand for the napkin. "Let me see." But instead of tossing the bundle into the nearby waste can, Molly examined the cloth, then wrapped it in the napkin and tucked it into her handbag.

"What are you doing?" Carol asked. "That's an odd souvenir."

Molly put a finger to her lips. "I'll tell you later." She stood, picking up her scraped-clean bowl. "Want to head back to the castle?"

Once they were driving away from the manor, Carol and Molly turned to Laura with inquiring expressions. "What happened during the tour?" Carol asked.

Laura shrugged. "I don't know. Maybe I imagined it." Now that a little time had passed, Laura wondered if she had exaggerated the portrait's likeness to Charlotte. But she hadn't made up the fact that Lord Sebastian didn't want visitors in the sitting room.

"Imagined what?" Molly asked. "Tell us and we can all decide."

"All right." Laura took a breath. "When I was being nosy and peeked inside that open door off the drawing room, I saw an old portrait that looked just like Charlotte Martin."

The hum of tires on the pavement was the only sound for a long moment.

"I know I probably imagined it," Laura said. "Plus, people often have similar features, right?"

"Wow." Molly exhaled in a whoosh. "It all makes sense. Charlotte went to visit Lord Sebastian, revealed she was a relative, and he killed her."

Her blunt statement startled disbelieving laughs out of Carol and Laura. "That's quite a leap," Carol said. "From a painting to murder." She signaled and slowed to turn into the castle entrance. "But maybe

Charlotte was related somehow. And she was using that as inspiration for her screenplay."

"I don't know what the laird's involvement is," Laura said, "but he didn't want me going in that room. I didn't see anything else out of the ordinary in there. It was a small sitting room, that's all." She thought back to the night of the reception. "I don't know if you noticed, but at the reception, Lord Sebastian acted like he'd never met Charlotte. And she went along with it."

"That was the same day she went to visit him, which is why it was so weird that they pretended not to know each other," Molly said.

"Maybe they had a disagreement during their visit," Carol suggested. "Hence the cold shoulder."

"Speaking of weird," Laura said, changing the subject. "Why did you save that dirty piece of cloth?"

Molly shrugged. "I thought it might be a clue." When both women raised their brows, she said, "No harm in keeping it, just in case."

Carol eased the car into a parking space and turned off the engine. "You're right, Molly. Good call." They climbed out of the car and strolled toward the castle entrance.

"Let's have a quiet evening tonight," Laura suggested. "I need to keep reading Charlotte's notebook and the screenplay." She held a hand out to Molly. "Let me have that piece of cloth to keep everything together." Molly handed it over and Laura slid it inside her small purse.

"What can we do to help?" Carol asked, opening the front door for her friends.

"How about looking through *Burke's Peerage*?" Laura suggested. "Find out more about Lord Sebastian's lineage." She pointed at Molly. "And you're still on social media watch."

"I can do that," Molly said. "But guess what? An episode of *A Highland Lass* is streaming tonight at nine. Want to watch it together?"

Carol gestured toward a handwritten sign on a stand next to the front desk that advertised a watch party in the den that evening. "Perhaps with some of our newest friends?"

The trio laughed, and Molly said, "I guess great minds think alike."

The women agreed to attend, then dispersed to their rooms. The first thing Laura did was kick off her shoes. They were adorable, but one of the straps bit into her foot at the wrong angle. She changed into her jeans and sat cross-legged on the bed with Charlotte's notebook and the screenplay.

The notebook was hard to follow, with pages of scribbling in Charlotte's distinctive scrawl. Many of the notes were regarding plot points Laura recognized from the screenplay, while others concerned facts about Scottish history. Charlotte seemed especially interested in the laws of inheritance.

Then she spotted the name MacVail—more specifically, Archibald and Malcolm, with birth dates. *Interesting. Charlotte was researching Lord Sebastian's family.* Laura made a note to ask Carol if *Burke's Peerage* had any information.

Laura's phone rang. She quickly snatched it up and answered.

"Nice hat," Brody greeted her.

"What do you mean?" she said, laughing. "I'm not wearing a hat."

"You are in this picture I'm looking at," Brody said. "You three clean up nicely. And what a setting!"

Molly must have posted pictures from the garden party. One of the other guests had snapped a shot of the three of them on the terrace.

"Yes, it's quite a place. We were at Lord Sebastian MacVail's garden party."

"Having tea and crumpets?" he asked.

"Strawberries and cream, actually." Laura suddenly felt like a cup of tea. She slid off the bed and switched on the electric kettle.

"Well, you have some anxious customers waiting for you to come home," Brody announced. "All the comments on your photos are either people wishing they were with you or wondering when you're coming back to reopen your bakery."

"This trip is memorable for sure, but I know I'll be happy to be home," Laura said.

"Ready to practice all the new baking techniques you're learning from the famed Agnes McVie?"

Laura faltered, not wanting to admit that she didn't feel she'd learned much of anything from Agnes aside from the fact that the celebrity chef wasn't nearly as warm and charming as she appeared on TV.

"Don't tell me," Brody went on, filling the silence left by Laura's hesitation. "You know everything already, right? Or better yet, you've been skipping class to investigate Charlotte Martin's murder."

Laura chuckled. "You're not far off the mark."

"Anything new?"

"Not really," she admitted. "But listen to this." She told him about the portrait, then about Charlotte's screenplay and the actress's visit to the manor house.

"Give me a break, sis. Secret heirs are the stuff of novels, not real life." Brody had always been a skeptic, a handy trait for an attorney. "You don't seriously think she was related to the MacVail family, do you?"

Laura glanced at the pages of the screenplay scattered about the bed. "Actually, I was kind of thinking that. I found mention of MacVail relatives in Charlotte's notes."

"Maybe she was just using them as inspiration."

Laura could go along with that theory except for one thing—the painting. "But that doesn't explain why a former Lady MacVail looks like she could be Charlotte's twin," she said. "And Lord Sebastian didn't want me to see it. He practically shut the door in my face." She switched off the kettle, which was whistling, and put a tea bag into a mug.

"I'll admit that is strange. But maybe he didn't want to acknowledge a relationship with Charlotte, whatever it is. Probably a distant cousin or something."

"That's what I thought." Frustration gnawed at Laura. "But right now, we don't know enough to say for sure." Careful not to splash, she poured hot water into the mug.

"I do know one thing," Brody said. "Inheritance laws are complicated in Scotland. Especially with titles and who they can be passed down to. Usually the oldest son inherits, then his son, and so forth."

"Una, the owner of the tea shop in the village, was explaining some of that."

"I'm sure a local would know more than me," Brody said, then paused. "Sorry, I've got another call. Talk tomorrow?"

"Sounds good." Laura disconnected the call, then dunked the tea bag in the hot water, thinking that maybe they would know something by then. Poor Terry, sitting in a jail cell. Maybe they should go visit him.

Laura was carrying her mug across the room when a scratching sound caught her attention. Surely the castle had mice . . . but that sounded like a pretty large mouse.

She stopped dead in the middle of the floor and listened, her ears straining. There it was again. This time she was able to tell where it was originating.

Behind the secret door.

15

Laura froze, adrenaline coursing through her. *Someone is back there, trying to get into my room.* Torn between confronting the intruder and going for backup, she glared at the secret door. Decision made, she ran out into the hall, then banged on Molly's door. "Molly, are you in there?"

The door flew open and Molly stood there, regarding Laura with wide eyes. "What's wrong? Is someone hurt?"

Carol peeked out of her room. "Who's banging on doors?" She saw her friends and slipped out, leaving the door ajar. "What's going on?"

"There's someone behind the secret door." Unable to suppress a shiver, Laura wrapped her arms around her torso.

"Let's go see," Carol said, leading the way. When she reached Laura's door, she turned and put a finger to her lips. All three women tiptoed inside.

Laura momentarily worried they wouldn't hear the sound and think she was imagining things. But as they stood on the carpet, ears straining, they all heard the faint scratching. Then it faded completely.

Carol ran to the wall, feeling around on the paneling. "How do you get through? I want to see who it was."

Laura showed them how to move the mechanism.

"Are you sure we should go in there?" Molly asked, and rightfully so—the pitch-black enclosure was far from welcoming.

"Yes," Laura said firmly. "There are three of us and probably one of them." She retrieved her phone from the bed and turned on the flashlight, and Carol and Molly followed suit with their phones.

The trio crowded through the narrow doorway into the hidden passage. In the pencil-point light from the phones, they could see a curved flight of stairs heading down. They shifted their beams to reveal another flight going up.

"Which way?" Laura asked. "Down?"

"Hold on," Carol said. "Before we go anywhere, we need to make sure we can get back into the bedroom." She grabbed a chair from the room and set it in the opening. "Don't want all three of us to get trapped."

Molly bit her lip. "Maybe we shouldn't do this. I don't want to die in here."

Carol sighed. "We aren't going to die." She jostled the chair, which barely budged. "This isn't going anywhere."

Laura thought of another thing. "I hate to say this now, Carol, but do you want to lock my door?" She pictured someone stealing in and moving the chair to trap them inside. But who? Wasn't everyone still at the garden party?

"Better safe than sorry." Carol slipped out of the enclosure into Laura's room and returned a few moments later. "All set. I turned the dead bolt too." That meant only someone with a key could get in, and as far as they knew, that was only Lady Freya or Lord Alan.

Laura took the first step down the stone staircase. The triangular treads were narrow and spiraled into darkness below. With every stair, she felt as if she were going deeper into the heart of the castle. No sound from outside penetrated the thick walls. The air was close and warm, a tiny breeze on her face the only reassurance that fresh air was trickling in. The other two were silent, focused on placing their feet.

The staircase continued to curve and the rectangle of light from her room disappeared, making the darkness fringing their feeble lights even thicker, almost tangible. Down and down they went, Laura losing count of the stairs.

They finally reached a landing, barely large enough to hold the three of them. Straight ahead was the outline of a door, rimmed in light, and to the left, another flight of stairs descended.

Laura's hand hovered over the door. "Want to see where this goes or keep going?"

"I think we've gone far enough for one day," Molly said. She edged closer to the next set of stairs. "I'll bet that goes down to the dungeons."

"I vote for stopping right here," Carol said. "Going underground could be dangerous."

"I agree." Laura's fingers found a latch, and when she pressed on it, the door swung open to reveal a pantry filled with canned goods. Through the open door, they heard a woman humming. While they watched, Mrs. Beasley crossed in front of the pantry door.

The trio ducked back, although Mrs. Beasley didn't spare the pantry a glance. Oven doors banged shut and dishes clattered. Then a man called, "Hello, the kitchen. The urns in the dining room need filling." A second later, director Clive O'Connor sauntered into view. "We're having a rather impromptu team meeting, so a tray of sandwiches wouldn't go amiss."

Mrs. Beasley murmured a response.

Laura hastily closed the door, careful not to make a sound. "Now we know where the first-floor entrance to the secret staircase is, at least."

"Do you think Mrs. Beasley was who we heard earlier?" Molly whispered.

Laura shrugged. "Maybe. But the kitchen isn't off-limits to guests, so it could have been anyone." Clive had certainly seemed at home, she thought, then said, "We haven't talked to Clive yet. Let's put him next on the list."

"And let's go see poor Terry," Carol said. "He's probably thinking he doesn't have a friend in the world."

Something clattered in the pantry, making them jump. Exchanging guilty looks, they hastened up the staircase.

The den, a room off the dining room, was packed with people when Laura went down for the broadcast of the show. She stood in the doorway a moment, trying to locate Carol and Molly. A hand went up in the back and she saw that they had saved her a seat between them on a sofa.

"There you are." Lord Alan strode across the carpet to Laura's side. "I was hoping to catch you. I made a copy of the map for you." He patted the pockets of his tweed jacket, then reached inside. "Ah, here it is." He handed her a folded piece of printer paper.

"Thanks," Laura said, unfolding the paper to take a peek. She was tempted to ask Lord Alan about the secret staircase, but hesitated. Lady Freya had warned them about the dangers of exploring. The castle's grounds were neatly drawn and labeled, including—what? Laura held the map closer. "Are those tunnels?"

Lord Alan glanced around, then put a hand on Laura's elbow, pulling her aside. "There are tunnels leading from the castle to the loch and to other buildings in the area. For smuggling, I believe, and for safety in times of war. But I must warn you, they are too dangerous to explore."

Laura laughed. She was adventurous, but even she had limits. "Don't worry. I have no intention of going underground."

The descending stairs we found earlier must connect to the tunnels. Laura studied the castle layout. Although rooms weren't labeled, the tunnel emerged from the castle near where she figured the kitchen was located.

"Are you going in to watch the show?" Lord Alan gestured for Laura to go first, his eyes twinkled. "I have to confess it's always exciting to see the old place on television."

As Laura nestled onto the couch between her friends, the evocative strains of a bagpipe sounded. A panorama of hills and loch appeared on the massive screen, and then the camera zoomed in toward the castle. Then the image faded out, and a shot of Charlotte sitting on a rock in a tartan cloak, hair blowing in the gentle breeze, replaced it. The words *A Highland Lass* gradually faded in.

In unison, the watchers—including the Glasgow women, Clive, Kyla, Finn, and Lord and Lady Cameron—sighed and murmured.

"She was a real beauty," one of the Glasgow women said.

Finn ducked his head, putting a hand to his forehead. Kyla stared at the screen, unmoving, while Clive's face twitched in a brief expression of annoyance.

Soon everyone was enraptured by the action on the screen, a scene between Charlotte and Finn. He looked to-die-for handsome, rakish curls dangling over his forehead and a lacy cravat at his throat. The pair gazed at each other, a perfect romantic moment made even more poignant by the realization that it had all gone so terribly wrong.

Gripped by the drama of the show, Laura was almost sad when the closing credits rolled. She couldn't wait to see the next episode. Around the room, the audience stood, stretching and chatting.

"That was lovely, that was," one of the Glasgow visitors said to Laura, the same who had spoken to her in the lobby. The woman pushed herself out of an overstuffed chair with a groan. "Are you coming to hear the big announcement about the show?"

"Big announcement?" This was news to Laura. She glanced over at Molly, the font of all show business information, but her friend merely shrugged.

"They're doing it in the dining room," the woman said. She picked up her knitting bag off the carpet and went to join her friends.

"I was planning on heading right up to my room." Carol suppressed a yawn. "But we'd better go find out what's going on."

"What did you two think of the show?" Molly's expression was eager. "It was one of their best episodes yet." Her face creased in a frown. "I'm so sad about Charlotte."

"Me too," Laura said, herding her friends toward the door. "It was really good. I was totally caught up and didn't want it to end."

Molly laughed. "Me neither. I'm going to buy the DVDs so I can watch it whenever I need a Scotland fix."

Voices and laughter echoed in the dining room, where the guests were grazing on assorted biscuits, cheese and crackers, and fruit. Tea and coffee were available, as well as Horlicks, a sweet malted drink served hot.

"Oh, I've heard of Horlicks," Molly said. "It's supposed to help you sleep."

"I'll have that, then," Carol said. "No more tea for me tonight."

Mugs of Horlicks in hand, the friends found a table and sat, watching the crowd. A few new faces had appeared, and since most were carrying cameras, Laura guessed they were from the media. The man Finn had accosted was there, giving the star a wide berth.

"All right, everyone," Clive said from his spot near the fireplace. Flanked by Kyla and Finn, the director stood with feet wide, hands clasped behind his back, and a satisfied smile on his face. "Thank you for coming tonight."

The talking subsided to a murmur and an air of expectation fell over the room. Laura spotted Agnes standing near Lady Freya and

Lord Alan. Mrs. Beasley hovered near the staff door, avid curiosity on her face.

"As you know," Clive began, "we tragically lost Charlotte Martin earlier this week." Flashbulbs went off, but the director ignored them. "Many of you have been wondering what would happen to *A Highland Lass* without our beautiful star." He ducked his head briefly in a gesture of sorrow and regret.

"He sure knows how to play an audience," Carol whispered in Laura's ear.

Laura agreed that the director's handling of the crowd and the situation was masterful, with no hint of turmoil or conflict on the show.

"You'll all be happy to hear my news," Clive continued. "Or at least I hope so, if you are enjoying the show."

At this prompting, shouts and cheers broke out, as if the crowd were reassuring him. One Glasgow guest stood and yelled, "We love you, Finn!" before being pulled down by her laughing friends.

"They're a lively bunch," Carol said, glancing over at the boisterous women.

"We love Finn too," Clive said smoothly. "And that's why you'll be glad to hear that he will remain with *A Highland Lass* next season as Ainslee's widower."

Everyone greeted this news with applause, and more flashbulbs went off as Finn inclined his head in acknowledgment. "I'm very happy to be part of the show," he said in his charming Scottish accent. "It's an honor and a pleasure."

"Now for our big news." Clive put his arm around Kyla. "Kyla Paterson will be moving into a leading role. Say hello to the new Highland lass!"

Kyla blushed deeply, a triumphant smile on her lips, as the reporters went wild, shouting questions and snapping shots.

The reporter Finn had argued with moved forward and shouted, "Is it true, Clive old man, that Charlotte was trying to get you fired?"

His question had the effect of drenching the crowd with cold water. For a moment there was confused silence. Rage flashed across Clive's normally bland features. Then, with a visible effort, he regained his poise. "Next question," he said, with a laugh. "No more questions about Charlotte, all right? Let her rest in peace."

As the reporters crowded closer, focused on Finn and Kyla, Clive gestured to one of the crew and whispered in his ear. The man went up to the argumentative reporter and said something that caused the journalist to storm out.

"What did you think of that?" Molly's eyes were round with shock. "What a rude question."

But a pertinent one. Laura wondered if Charlotte had complained about Clive to the network. Even if she had, he'd somehow managed to remain in control of the show. A chill ran down her spine. Maybe Charlotte had never had a chance to complain. Maybe the killer had gotten to her first.

Before going to bed, Laura blocked the secret door with one of the bureaus in her room. If she heard something behind the wall again, she would ask to change rooms. Carol's words echoed in her mind. *Better safe than sorry.*

16

"Mrs. Beasley is putting together a basket of treats," Lady Freya said. She shut the French door and crossed the terrace to where the three friends were sitting in the warm morning sun. "I can't believe I didn't think of visiting poor Terry sooner."

Laura glanced up from her copy of the garden map. "You've had a lot on your plate the last few days, Lady Freya. I'm sure he understands."

"Besides, didn't you engage a solicitor for him?" Carol asked. "That was extremely helpful."

Lady Freya sighed, gazing at the garden with a forlorn expression. "What will really help is clearing his name."

"We're working on it," Laura said. "There seem to be several prospective motives to follow. One is Charlotte's tension with Clive, the second her breakup with Finn, and the third is her potential relationship to Lord Sebastian's family."

Their hostess made a scoffing sound. "That's not possible. Lord Sebastian is the only surviving member of the MacVails of Glenellen."

Molly raised a finger. "Or so everyone thinks. Carol studied *Burke's Peerage* last night and found there was an older son, Malcolm. Sebastian's father was Archibald."

Lady Freya's brow furrowed. "But Malcolm died in the war. Or went missing, actually. His body was never found."

"That's right," Laura said. "His plane went down during World War II." Over breakfast, Carol and Molly had shared what they had gleaned from *Burke's Peerage* and research online. "There must be more to the family history."

"Or Charlotte believed her own story." Lady Freya sounded as if she favored that theory. She waved a dismissive hand. "But it's all moot now."

Unless Charlotte's theory had led to murder. But Laura didn't bother to argue the point. Lady Freya's attitude was understandable, since the idea of secret heirs was the stuff of fiction.

Laura rattled the map. "We're getting ready to explore the gardens, Lady Freya. Would you care to give us a tour?"

"What do you have there?" their hostess asked.

Laura showed off the map. "His lordship gave me a copy."

"I'd love to show you around," Lady Freya said. "Our plan is to restore all the garden features. That's why I need dear Terry. He was my right hand."

A muffled bark sounded followed by scratching on glass, and they all turned to see Minnie pressing her nose against the glass of the French door.

Lady Freya laughed. "I swear she has bat ears. All I have to do is say the word 'garden' and she's right there, eager to go."

After being let out of the house, Minnie accompanied them down the stone steps into the garden.

"What have you seen so far?" Lady Freya asked. Laura mentioned the spots they had visited. "But you haven't seen the lily pond? All right, come this way."

Without even glancing at the map, Lady Freya led them through a thicket of purple rhododendrons onto a narrow footpath. "Those bushes used to line the path," she said. "Now they smother it."

They pushed through the hedges, a faint trace of gravel underfoot the only marker of the once wider path. Laura examined the map to orient herself as they wound up an incline and then circled back down around. Minnie sidled past the women and took a position in the lead, as if to show them the way.

The pond was actually an oval, man-made pool lined with hewn blocks and edged by a brick surround. The water was putrid, with leaves and petals from overhanging magnolia trees littering the water. A cluster of yellow irises grew at one end, and lily pads filled the other end. Lichen-covered statues stood here and there in overgrown flower beds.

"The inlets and outlets are mostly blocked," Lady Freya said. "That's why the water is stagnant. Fixing it was next on our list."

They all remained a distance from the edge to avoid the almost overwhelming odor of rotting plants and decay. But Laura could imagine how inviting the pond would be once the water flowed fresh again.

"Where's Minnie?" Lady Freya asked suddenly. She whistled. "Minnie, come."

The dog returned with a crash. She burst through the bushes and trotted toward her mistress. Lady Freya patted her head. "What do you have in your mouth? Minnie, drop it."

The dog's massive jaws opened and a rectangular object fell out onto the bricks. It was a cell phone with a pink alligator case. Charlotte's phone.

"May I?" Molly asked Lady Freya. At her ladyship's nod, Molly used a tissue to pick up the phone. "The battery still has life," she announced. "And look."

The screen she turned to face them displayed a message. *Charlotte, so glad you're joining us for next season's* Brides of Edinburgh Castle. *Your agent is in receipt of your contract.*

"So Charlotte was moving to a new show," Laura said. "I haven't heard of that one."

"It's another historical show. On a rival network, no less." Lady Freya's tone was tart. "So she *was* jumping ship."

"Looks that way," Carol said. "The question is, who knew about this?"

Laura relayed the conversation she had overheard between Kyla and Clive. "So Kyla knew for sure, and she tried to warn Clive."

"Do you think that, on top of Charlotte's threats to complain about Clive to the network, the news about her leaving pushed him over the edge?" Molly asked.

Lady Freya appeared horrified. "You mean a murderer could be staying in my castle?" She glanced back through the woods toward the castle as though there might be a visible sign. "But he seems like such a nice man. So sophisticated and worldly."

Despite her brave words about clearing Terry, Lady Freya obviously hadn't thought through the implications—namely that someone else was guilty. Someone she probably knew.

Carol patted their hostess on the arm in a comforting manner. "We're only speculating right now. And as long as we keep these conversations between us, we'll all be safe."

Her ladyship made a motion in front of her lips as if locking them with a key. "I won't say a word to anyone, not even Lord Alan. He often speaks without thinking, I'm afraid."

"We'd better call the police," Laura said. "They will need to collect Charlotte's phone as evidence." She glanced around. "And we might have to wait here until they come. They could want to search this area." Laura grimaced at the thought. It wasn't exactly the best spot to wait, near the fetid pond under thick, overhanging trees.

Lady Freya patted her pockets. "I didn't bring my phone. Do you have one I can use?"

Carol handed over her phone, and Lady Freya placed a call to Inspector Gough.

"Yes, Inspector," Lady Freya said. "We found Charlotte Martin's cell phone. Well, actually my dog did." Minnie gazed adoringly at her mistress and wagged her tail at the mention of her name. "Somewhere in the bushes near the lily pond. All right. We'll meet you at the castle." She returned Carol's phone to her. "Since we don't know the exact spot Minnie found the phone, we're free to go back up."

After they spoke to Inspector Gough, the trio hopped in the rental car for the visit to Terry. Mrs. Beasley had packed a hamper full of treats, and they loaded that into the back seat beside Laura. It was Molly's turn to ride shotgun.

The route to the police station took them to the other side of Glenellen, on the main road to Fort William. "This isn't exactly a planned stop on my tour of Scotland," Molly murmured when they pulled in.

"Mine either," Laura said, studying the nondescript brick building. It looked like police stations everywhere—modern, municipal, and rather unattractive.

Constable Hail was standing near the front desk when they entered, speaking to the dispatcher. She looked up with a smile of recognition. "How may I help you today, ladies?" she asked.

"We're here to see Terry," Laura said, realizing that she didn't even know his last name.

"Terry Cameron?" Her eyes fell on the hamper. "Let me take a look." Once she searched through the biscuits and cake and sandwiches, she gestured. "Right this way." She came around the desk and led them to a side door, opening it to reveal a corridor.

"He has the same name as the lord and lady," Molly said in confusion. "But he's the gardener and they live in the castle."

"Different branch of the clan," Constable Hail said, overhearing. "Everything comes down through the lineage. And if you're a distant cousin, well, you're out of luck, aren't you?" She unlocked another door, allowing them to precede her. It shut behind them with a clang.

Dim fluorescent lights flickered overhead, and to their left was a jail cell. No one was inside. Constable Hail led them to a second cell, which also contained a bunk bed and a couple of chairs.

"You've got visitors, Terry," the constable said.

Terry had been lounging on the lower bunk, but now he rolled out and stood. His eyes lit up. "Good morning, ladies." He sketched a bow, pretending to doff a nonexistent hat.

"Good morning to you," Laura said. "We've brought treats from the castle."

"There isn't a file in the cake, though," Molly said, then sent a sheepish look at the constable. "Just kidding."

The officer took the joke in good grace, since it probably wasn't the first time she had heard it. "I'll be out in the office. Ring the buzzer when you're ready." She pointed to a button near the door.

After the door clicked shut behind Constable Hail, Terry said, "They're not treating me bad in here. But it's rough being locked up inside, away from my garden." His face was mournful.

"I'll bet," Laura said. "Lady Freya showed us the lily pond today and told me about your plans."

"It will be lovely when we're done." His eyes darkened. "If I ever see it again."

Carol opened the hamper and showed him the treats, then handed him a packet of biscuits through the bars. "We're trying to figure out who killed Charlotte. We found her cell phone down by the pond. Well, actually Minnie did."

"Minnie's a good 'un." Terry opened the packet and held it out to them politely. When they shook their heads, he took a biscuit and bit into it. "So you ladies are looking into things. Any ideas yet?"

Laura thought it wise not to speculate, and she saw by her friends' expressions that they agreed. "We're keeping open minds right now, Terry. But we were hoping you might be able to help us."

"I'm not sure how." With a shrug, he removed another biscuit. "But I can tell you this. Someone took my scarf, right off the hook in my cottage. The police don't believe me."

The scarf that's now considered primary evidence of his guilt, Laura thought grimly. "Was the cottage locked?"

He shook his head. "No. Never. No one has ever bothered it before. I don't have much of value, you see." He cracked a grin. "Unless you want gardening tools."

"You didn't leave it somewhere, maybe?" Laura asked. "Like on a garden bench or up at the castle?" At his denial, she realized that someone must have slipped into his cottage and grabbed it. Which meant they probably wanted to frame him. Laura felt sick at the idea of such evil forethought.

Carol took over the questioning. "Did you see anything unusual that night? Overhear any conversations or arguments? From what we can figure, quite a few people were moving about the grounds."

Terry thought for a long moment. "Hold on. I did see someone, but with all the visitors at the reception, I really didn't give it much thought. Someone was walking through the grounds wearing a hooded cloak."

Laura's heart sank. "Charlotte had on a cloak. Black velvet."

"This one was tartan. One of those used in the television show. That same plaid."

Terry didn't have anything else to add, but he promised to "rack my brains," as he put it. Before the women left, he scrawled thank-you notes, asking them to hand-deliver the messages to Lady Freya and Mrs. Beasley.

"Are you thinking what I'm thinking?" Carol asked Laura as they drove away from the police station.

"Yes," Laura said. Then she laughed. "Well, I assume so. I'm wondering if that strip of cloth Minnie found matches one of those cloaks."

Now in the back for the return ride, Molly leaned forward between the seats. "That won't prove who was wearing it."

"That's true," Laura said. "But every little piece of the puzzle will hopefully add up to the big picture. Maybe someone saw the person in the cloak but didn't think anything of it. The police can question everyone again. I'm pretty sure they requested the guest list from the reception, including contact information."

At the castle, they found Lady Freya at the desk. "The police were very pleased about the phone," she reported, smiling at her dog, flopped on the carpet beside her. "They were joking about hiring Minnie as an auxiliary officer."

Laura laughed, then handed her the notes. "From Terry. As for Minnie, they're definitely going to want to hire her." She unzipped the side pocket of her handbag, where she had tucked the strip of cloth. "She brought me this at the garden party."

Lady Freya stared at the muddy tartan. "Where did she get that? It's not Charlotte's, is it?"

"Charlotte was wearing a black cloak," Carol said. She lowered her voice. "But Terry said he saw someone in plaid."

"Like the ones they wear on *A Highland Lass*?" Lady Freya gestured. "Let's check the dressing rooms."

That was easy. Laura had been wondering how they could access the show's wardrobe.

As they followed Lady Freya to yet another wing of the castle, her ladyship said, "By the way, Lord Sebastian called to invite you three to tea. I tentatively accepted for you. I hope that was all right."

"Of course," Molly said. "We'll go over after the baking lesson." They were scheduled for an early afternoon lesson while Agnes worked with the new students this morning to get them caught up.

What does Lord Sebastian want? I wonder if we could get him to discuss the portrait or Charlotte's visit.

Lady Freya opened a door and flicked on a light to reveal a large room crammed with rolling racks of clothing. "These rooms used to be offices for the estate, back when they had a steward, gamekeeper, head stableman, and the like."

"Having the television crew work here must be a nice boost." Laura scanned the clothing, looking for the distinctive tartan, but her eyes nearly crossed with the effort. There was so much plaid, as was to be expected in a Scottish costume drama.

"It has been," Lady Freya said. "And we've had some nibbles from a movie production company about filming a romance here." She began to browse through clothing. "But until we solve Charlotte's death ..."

"Let's hope we figure it out soon," Molly said sympathetically.

"Over here," Carol called. "I think I've found it." She held up a tartan cloak with a muddy hem—and it was missing a piece on the bottom.

Carol laid the cloak across a table, then the women watched as Laura carefully matched the strip Minnie found with the cloak.

"Yes, this is the one. Your instincts were right, Molly." Laura took a picture of the garment with her phone. "Now we need to figure out who was wearing it."

"And if they had anything to do with Charlotte's death," Molly added.

A few hours later, after baking class, the friends discussed the cloak's significance while driving to the manor for tea with Lord Sebastian. "One main point is this," Carol said. "Who else confessed to being in the gardens that night? If the person is innocent, why wouldn't they come forward?"

Laura smiled at her friend with admiration. "I think you missed your calling, oh logical one." They had called Constable Hail about the cloak and its missing strip, but the policewoman had merely told them to hang on to the items. "I was pretty disappointed that the constable wasn't excited about our new evidence. She acted like it was irrelevant."

"That's because they're completely focused on Terry right now," Molly said. "I wonder who called in the tip about him being with Charlotte the night she died." The women had asked but the officer refused to share the name. "Maybe it was a case of mistaken identity. Maybe the cloak wearer was the killer. Or were they the witness?"

Carol rolled the rental car to a stop near the manor's front steps and braked. Today they were the only visitors. "Unfortunately, all we know is the person borrowed a cloak. The why is still up in the air."

No one answered when they rang the front bell. "That's strange," Molly said. "The invitation was for today, right?"

"Lady Freya said it was," Carol said. "Maybe he's out back and didn't hear the doorbell." She glanced at her watch. "We are a few minutes early."

The women located a side path and followed it around the house, which was a pleasant detour. Birds chirped and sang in bushes and hopped along the grass. Bees buzzed in rosebushes while a gentle breeze rustled in tall trees.

Lord Sebastian wasn't in the garden or on the terrace. "Let's try one last thing," Carol said. Following her lead, they climbed the stone stairs to the French doors, which stood open to the drawing room.

"He must be here." Laura put her head inside the open door and called, "Lord Sebastian, are you home?"

The laird's response was a loud groan of pain.

17

"What was that?" Molly cried in concern. "Is he ill?"

Laura didn't stop to ask questions. She pushed on the French door and entered the drawing room with Carol and Molly on her heels. The nobleman was in his seventies and sudden illness wasn't out of the question.

"Lord Sebastian?" Laura called again, gazing around the empty room. The door to the small sitting room was open, so she hurried in that direction. To her shock and dismay, the laird was sprawled on the carpet, right in front of the mysterious portrait. She broke into a run and soon reached his side.

Molly gasped. "Is that blood?" She pointed to a stain on the carpet.

"I think so." Biting her lip, Laura hunkered down beside the stricken man. His hair was matted with blood and his skin had a horrible gray tinge. "Carol, call 999. It looks like someone attacked him."

Carol immediately made the call. Molly swept her gaze around the room, her face creased with fear. She moved closer to Carol. "What if the attacker is still here somewhere?"

"There are three of us," Laura said. "We'll be all right." She checked Lord Sebastian's pulse, relieved to feel it strong under her fingertips. He groaned again, moving his arms and legs. "Stay still, Lord Sebastian. Help is on the way."

His face screwed up in pain, then he blinked a few times and opened his eyes. She watched as he struggled to focus on her face. "Laura?" He strained to sit up. "I invited you all to tea."

Laura gently pushed on his shoulders, trying to get him to relax. "Don't worry about that right now."

"They're on their way." Carol put away her phone. "I'm going out front to wait."

Laura kept an eye on Lord Sebastian, refusing to let him get up despite his attempts to do so. A few minutes later, she was relieved to hear the sound of voices as the medics accompanied Carol into the room, Constable Hail trailing behind.

An examination revealed that the injury looked worse than it was. "You're fortunate, your lordship," a female medic said, applying a bandage to the injury. "It was only a glancing blow."

"Head wounds do bleed a lot," the other said. He reeled off a list of symptoms to watch for as his partner finished up. "No sign of concussion yet, but it's nothing to mess with," he concluded.

While the medics worked, Carol and Molly had gone to the kitchen to make tea. They entered now, Carol lugging a tray. Molly cleared a table so she could set it down.

"Do you want a cup of tea before you go?" Carol asked the medics.

"No, we'd better get back to the station," the woman said. "A call could come in any moment." She patted Lord Sebastian on the shoulder. "Be sure to call your general practitioner for a follow-up. And let us know if you have any concerning symptoms."

Carol poured tea while Constable Hail settled in to ask questions. She began with the three friends, asking them why they were at the manor and what they'd seen. This gave Lord Sebastian additional time to recover. He was sipping tea on a sofa, the bandage giving him a rakish air, when the policewoman asked him to tell her what had happened.

"That's the rub," Lord Sebastian said. "I don't know. I was standing in this room when *wham*—something hit me. That's the last thing I remember until I saw this lovely lady's face looking down at me." He nodded at Laura.

The constable's brow furrowed as she considered this. "Were you expecting another guest?"

"No, only these three ladies," he said. "My cleaner was here earlier, but she was long gone before the incident."

"We'll need to speak to your cleaner." Constable Hail took down the name and contact information. She set aside her notes. "I'm going to take a look around, if you don't mind." She examined every nook of the room, but came up empty-handed. Apparently not dissuaded by this, she proceeded into the drawing room. She was probably trying to find the weapon, Laura guessed.

They sipped tea while waiting for the constable to finish her search. Laura kept glancing at the portrait, and every time, she saw a stronger resemblance to Charlotte. She hadn't imagined it. Nor had she imagined the plotline in Charlotte's screenplay. Carol and Molly kept watching the painting as well.

"No luck, I'm afraid," Constable Hail said. "Whoever it was must have carried the weapon away. Still, I'll file a report of the assault." She scanned the room one final time. "You may want to install an alarm system."

Lord Sebastian's expression soured. "That would be quite an insult for the old place. We've withstood wars and famines and sieges, and now I need an alarm system? No thank you."

"It's a different world, I'm afraid." Constable Hail issued a sympathetic smile. "I'll be off. But please don't hesitate to call if you need us."

Carol showed the officer to the door and after she returned, Laura decided to take the bull by the horns, so to speak. "Lord Sebastian, that portrait." She tipped her chin toward the painting. "That woman and Charlotte Martin could be twins."

"Really, it's true," Molly said, getting up and approaching the painting. "The shape of her face, especially the chin. And those eyes."

Lord Sebastian finished his tea, a small smile on his lips. "I noticed it too, when Charlotte came to visit me. Lady Isla MacVail. She lived here in the early 1800s."

"Was Charlotte related to you?" Laura all but blurted. She watched the laird carefully to see if he flinched at her words.

But Lord Sebastian calmly held his cup out for Carol to fill. "The jury was still out on that one, although I wouldn't have minded. She had quite a tale to tell, you see. She claimed she was the great-granddaughter of Malcolm MacVail."

"The pilot who went down in World War II," Carol said. At the laird's surprised glance, she flushed. "We've been browsing through *Burke's Peerage*."

"As I said, that's what she told me," Lord Sebastian said. "However, there is no record of a marriage here. Charlotte said he married in France during the war, but after he disappeared, his widow never pursued a claim against the estate." His furrowed brow conveyed doubt.

Laura considered this story of a hasty wartime marriage in a foreign country and a grieving widow reluctant to face an intimidating situation. "What do you think, Lord Sebastian? Was she right?"

He studied the portrait as though it held answers. "I don't know. She resembled Lady Isla, that is true. But she hadn't found any definitive proof that I was aware of, and we agreed to keep it entirely private until it was proven."

Laura exchanged glances with her friends. *That must be why they acted like strangers at the party.*

"She did float the idea of a DNA test," Lord Sebastian said, then fell silent.

"Would you have done it?" Carol asked after a moment.

"I probably would have." His smile was grim. "I'm the last of the line, you see. Although, being a woman, Charlotte couldn't have inherited this particular title, she could have taken over the manor. I have no idea what will happen to the property when I'm gone."

"There are no other relatives?" Molly asked. "How sad."

He set his cup down with a clink. "I'm afraid not. All the legitimate heirs died without issue, even some distant cousins in Canada."

The idea of a long and storied lineage coming to an end was a sad one. And the actress might have been a comfort to Lord Sebastian in his older years as well.

Then a terrible realization gripped Laura. If there were no heirs to the estate, why had someone attacked Lord Sebastian?

After making sure his lordship was all right to be left alone, the women returned to the castle, where they changed into casual clothing before gathering in Laura's room to chat.

"It's a good thing we showed up when we did," Carol said. "I hate to think of him lying on the carpet for hours."

Molly shuddered. "We probably missed the assailant by minutes."

"So how did they get away without us spotting them?" Laura asked. "We didn't see another car. And when we went around the house, I didn't see anyone on the grounds or in the fields by the loch."

"Maybe they went the other way, toward the village," Carol said.

Standing by the window, Laura spotted a tall figure strolling through the garden. "Finn is alone. Want to go talk to him?"

"Yes, let's," Molly said. "There's a lot we still don't know, and he's a good place to start."

"Or a good-looking place to start," Carol said wryly.

They found Finn down by the loch, bailing out a rowboat with an old can.

"Good afternoon, ladies," he said. The actor wore a melancholy air like a garment, revealed in the slump of his broad shoulders and the smile that didn't reach his eyes.

"That's good news about the show continuing," Molly said. She gulped, looking as if she wished she could retract her remark. "I mean, it will never be the same without Charlotte, but still…" Her words trailed off.

"It's fortunate for those of us who need the work." Finn set the bailing can aside and picked up a large sponge. "I'm thrilled for my sister, of course. She's been wanting a bigger role for a while."

Laura glanced at her friends. Was that a motive to kill the person standing in her way? Did Kyla have an alibi? How could they find out?

"One piece of good news," Finn said. "I'm officially off the hook." He squeezed the sponge into the water. "I stopped to get gas on my way to Edinburgh."

"And they got a copy of the receipt?" Carol guessed.

"Even better. They had security camera footage." He cracked a grin. "The attendant tried to sell it to a tabloid, but the police took it into evidence."

Laura wondered if it was the same reporter Finn had intercepted on the cliffs. Encouraged by his openness, she said, "Charlotte was fine when you left her. Any idea what happened after?"

Finn pushed the sponge into the bottom of the boat. "I've been racking my brain day and night. I don't believe it was that gardener chap."

"We don't either," Molly said. "And guess what? He saw someone else in the garden. Not you, unless you were wearing a cloak."

The actor laughed. "No, I wasn't wearing a cloak." He squeezed out the sponge again then tossed it into the boat, a signal he was almost ready to push off. "I wouldn't have left her if I'd known." His head dropped. "I have to live with that the rest of my life."

"We always have regrets when we lose someone we love," Molly said, and Laura knew she was thinking about her late husband, Kevin, who had died from a rare reaction to an antibiotic. "But it does get better in time."

Finn raised his head. "You understand, don't you?" When Molly nodded, he said, "We were over as a couple, and I finally accepted it that night. But I'll always love her."

"I'm sure she knows," Molly said, her voice still soft. After a pause, she shifted course slightly. "We were at Lord Sebastian's today. He said that Charlotte might be a long-lost relative."

Finn didn't appear surprised by this news. "She was really obsessed with her family history lately. I didn't know the details, but she said she was almost ready to share some major news." He picked up an oar and slid it into the oarlock.

Laura wondered who else knew about her quest. "We won't keep you," she said, seeing he was eager to begin his row. "But do you have any thoughts who could have been wearing that cloak? It belonged to the show."

"You three are wee detectives, are you?" Finn's grin said he was more amused than bothered. "I really don't know. Most of the technical crew had left. And Kyla and Clive went down to the pub for a karaoke night. Now, if you'll excuse me . . ."

"Of course," Carol said. "Thank you for not minding our nosiness and answering our questions."

"Whatever it takes to get justice for Charlotte," he said.

They watched as Finn pushed off, leaped into the boat with athletic grace, and began to row across the loch. He made quite the picture with his windblown hair and strong arms pulling on the oars as he skimmed across blue water. At least Molly seemed to think so.

"Molly." Laura tugged at her friend's arm. "Earth to Molly."

"Sorry," Molly said. "I'm still a little starstruck, I guess."

Without discussion, the trio started walking along the path. "I think we should pay a visit to the pub," Laura said. "We can have dinner there."

"That's a thought," Carol said. "I'll tell Lady Freya that we won't be at the castle for dinner." She laughed at hearing her own words. "I still get a kick out of saying that." They stopped strolling for a minute while Carol placed the call.

"What did she say?" Molly asked when Carol hung up.

Carol slipped her phone into her bag. "She recommends the fresh-caught salmon and the steak pie."

Molly groaned, putting a hand to her midsection. "Both sound so good. I'm starving."

"Me too." Laura had anticipated eating at Lord Sebastian's, but after finding him stricken, they hadn't given food a second thought. She studied the manor as they walked by. "I hope Lord Sebastian will feel better soon."

"I do too." Carol's expression was troubled, but when she didn't comment further, Laura guessed she was deep in thought about the event.

"We can check in later," Laura said. "I'll sleep better if we do."

The evening air was soft and warm, and the village had a lively air. People strolled along the streets, grilled in their gardens, and played in the park. The Thistle and Oyster appeared busy, with patrons streaming in and out. Some diners sat on a side patio under strings of lights.

Inside, the pub had low ceilings, yellowed plaster walls, and a long gleaming bar. Flags, photographs, and artifacts such as swords and shields decorated the walls, giving the place character. By the crowd at the bar, Laura guessed they ordered there. "Tell me what you want," she said to her friends, pointing to a chalkboard menu. "I'll go order for us."

"And we'll go grab a table," Carol said.

After they decided, Laura joined the line and slowly worked her way to the front. An older man stood ready, pencil and order pad in hand. "What can I get ye?" he asked.

"Steak pie, salmon plate, and fish pie." Laura eyed a drink menu. Recognizing a popular local soft drink derived from elderflowers, she added, "And three glasses of sparkling pressé. We're out on the patio."

He nodded. "I'll get your drinks." He shouted to another server, who loaded a tray with three green bottles and three glasses.

Laura carried the tray through the pub, dodging tables and standing customers. At the glass doors leading to the patio, a man leaped forward and opened it for her. Glancing at him to say thanks, she recognized Clive, but he didn't seem to know her.

She sidled through the doorway and glanced around for her friends. They had a table in back, near a cedar hedge and a half barrel filled with bright flowers.

"Guess who I saw," she said, handing around the bottles and glasses. "Clive. I guess he comes here a lot."

"I can see why," Molly said. "It seems like a fun place." As if to underline her words, a group of women at the next table let out a peal of laughter.

The three women clinked their glasses in a toast, then sipped and people-watched. Carol picked up her phone. "I keep thinking about some things I want to research. But I'm not sure if they're related."

"That's no surprise." Laura shook her head. "There are so many clues pointing in different directions. What are you wondering?"

"Remember Una from the café?" Carol asked. "She mentioned that more than one woman from the castle had been looking for information about her family. And then Lord Sebastian was hit on the head. He also has no heirs."

Laura's eyebrows went up. "You think there is someone else who might be related?"

"Or thinks they are." Carol continued to search. After a few minutes, she gave a grunt of satisfaction. "Guess what? Agnes McVie's

Italian grandmother moved from the Fort William area to Glasgow in the 1940s. What if there is a Glenellen connection?"

"I'm not sure what that would prove," Laura said. "But we can follow up with Una." She glanced toward the pub doors and saw the landlord, as the owner was called, coming their way with plates.

The landlord set the plates down, retrieving utensils rolled in napkins from his pocket. Then he checked the table, making sure they had everything. "Do you need anything else?" he asked with a friendly smile.

"This looks—and smells—great," Laura said. "But I do have a question, if you have a minute."

He checked over his shoulder and, seeming satisfied that all was under control, nodded. "Go ahead."

"We're staying at the castle," Laura explained. "And at Lady Freya's request, we're trying to help poor Terry."

The mention of her ladyship and the gardener made the landlord straighten up. "Do tell," he said. "It's a crying shame they locked that bloke behind bars. What can I do for you?"

Laura craned her neck to make sure Clive wasn't within earshot. He was still inside the pub, talking to a couple of men from his crew. "I understand some people from the television show were here the night Charlotte died." She intentionally kept the question open-ended, hoping to glean more information.

"And so they were." The landlord tipped his chin toward the pub. "The director is making it his life's work to close us down every night. Under lots of stress, apparently."

"What about the stars?" Laura asked.

"The only one here that night was Kyla. She and Clive sang songs on karaoke together. She wasn't bad, but him?" The landlord grimaced and pretended to clean out an ear. "Even the cats ran off."

The ladies chuckled. "So did Kyla close the place down?" Laura asked, holding her breath for the answer.

With a headshake, he picked up the tray, ready to return to his work. "No, she left early. She claimed she had a headache."

18

Kyla left early? Maybe she had gone to meet Charlotte after leaving the pub. "Do you remember what time?" Laura asked.

Gazing upward, the landlord gave it some thought. "Around ten, I think." He glanced around the table. "Is there anything else? I really should get back to it."

"Sorry to keep you," Laura said. "Thanks." She picked up her fork, ready to dig into the perfectly browned mashed potato topping on her fish pie, which smelled wonderful.

"Give us a shout if you need anything." The landlord bustled away, pausing at a nearby table to check on the diners.

"Want to try the salmon?" Molly cut the thick fillet into several pieces. She passed her plate around, and Laura and Carol did the same with their entrées.

As the meal went on, Laura felt herself relax. The pub was lively, with happy patrons and traditional Celtic music piped over a loudspeaker, but here in the corner, they ate in peace. They were thinking about dessert when a woman at a nearby table got up. She was dressed in a big hat and sunglasses, despite the fact it was almost evening. But as she exited the patio, her face was visible for a moment.

Kyla. Laura's skin tingled. What had the actress overheard? Had she been sitting there when they asked the landlord about karaoke night? Oh, she hoped not.

Carol nudged Laura with a grimace, letting her know she also noticed the actress.

After paying the check, the women strolled down the lane toward the tearoom.

"If they're closed already, we'll have to come back tomorrow," Carol said. "But I tell you, I can use the extra walk after that meal."

"Me too," Laura said. The fish pie had been excellent and so had the other dishes. The steak pie's light and flaky crust had been superb.

"At least we're achieving our main goal here, ladies," Molly said brightly, "which was sampling authentic Scottish dishes for inspiration. In case you forgot."

"Oh, I'm inspired," Laura reassured her friends. "I've been brainstorming all week. When we haven't been chasing clues, that is. I can't wait to get home and try out my ideas."

"And we can't wait for you to do that either." Carol threaded her arms through Laura's and Molly's. "What a lovely night."

The setting sun tinted the whitewashed houses gold, and on the loch, gilded waves rippled. As they made their way down the lane, they found lights still on in The Library Tearoom. The front door stood open.

"Now I want dessert," Laura said, tempted by a glimpse of the pastry case. "More inspiration, of course."

Una was working behind the counter. "*Guid evenin*. How are you ladies?"

"Great," Molly said. "We're here for a cup of tea and dessert." She patted her midsection. "Nothing too big since we just came from the pub."

"Och, he puts on a good spread, he does." Una opened the door of a small, clear cabinet on top of the main case. "What you want is a piece of tablet. A bit of sweet to put the perfect finish on a meal."

"I can't wait to try it," Laura said. She had perfected her own tablet recipe for Bread on Arrival, but she was eager to sample the tearoom's version of the treat, which combined sugar, butter, and condensed milk into a fudge-like candy.

Una made a shooing motion. "You go ahead to your table and I'll be right over."

The women sat at their usual spot in the corner, and Una brought over cups of herbal tea and a small plate with three pieces of dense golden tablet. A family group came in, so the café owner went to wait on them.

Laura nibbled a corner of the candy, which tasted of vanilla and caramel and melted on her tongue. "This is incredible."

"It's almost as good as yours, Laura," Carol said generously.

Laura thought for a moment. "I wouldn't say better or worse, just slightly different. Tastes like Una uses another kind of vanilla."

In between small bites of tablet, Molly studied the photographs on the wall. "I wonder if Agnes's grandmother is in any of these."

"If I remember correctly, there's a photo of her on Agnes's website." Laura pulled out her phone and brought up the chef's *About* page. "Here she is."

The photograph of a comfortably plump woman standing at a bakery counter was cropped and grainy, but her features were fairly clear. Laura passed her phone to Carol, then glanced around the room at the dozens of pictures on the walls. "Now we have to scour these for a match." It was a daunting prospect.

Una returned to their table. "Would you like another round of tea?"

"I think we're all right, thank you," Carol said. "But if you have a moment, we've got a question for you. Do you recognize this woman?" She showed the bakery owner the photograph.

Una took the phone and studied the picture. "I do," she said, then set the phone down and stepped closer to the wall, squinting at the frames.

The Bakehouse Three exchanged excited glances.

"Here she is. Isabel Rico." Una pointed to a photograph of a large vegetable garden with several smiling people standing nearby. "That's the victory garden up at the manor. Fed most of the village out of that, they did. Isabel was the cook up at the manor then. See her? She's second from the left. And the man beside her is the old baron." Una indicated a portly man with a round head, a huge walrus mustache, and multiple chins. Laura thought his grandson, Lord Sebastian, had the same nose and brow.

They got up to take a better look. Molly grabbed Laura's phone and compared the picture online with the one on the wall. "So Agnes's grandmother not only lived in Glenellen, she lived at the manor."

The knot of exhilaration in Laura's belly informed her they were on to something, even if she wasn't quite sure what yet. Another interesting tidbit from Una floated into her mind. "Do you think her husband was interned? Or another family member?"

"Maybe so," Una said. "I can get the list for you. It's in the library." She held her hand out for the phone. "Do you mind if I check something?"

"Of course not," Molly said, giving the device to the older woman.

Una scrolled up the page, then issued a grunt of satisfaction. "There she is. That's the other woman who came in here seeking information on her family." Agnes's face smiled out at them from the professional headshot on her site. "She resembles her grandmother quite a lot, doesn't she?"

Another confirmation. Had Agnes held the cooking class at the castle so she could do family research in the village? That made sense.

"Maybe we will take another cup of tea," Carol said, returning to her seat.

"Coming right up. And I'll get you the list of internees." Una set down the phone and scooped up the empty teapot.

Laura was thankful Una didn't question why they were being so nosy about another woman's family. Maybe to a librarian, research was simply an acceptable form of snooping.

Over fresh, hot tea, they browsed through the binder Una gave them, which had neatly typed lists of names and other information, such as birth date, village, occupation, and internment dates.

"I can't believe this happened," Carol said. "These men were all citizens."

"It happened in the United States too," Molly said. "I'm sure the government thought they were being prudent."

Laura found the name she was looking for. "Angelo Rico, Glenellen. That's got to be him." She studied the entry, which said he had died in 1942 of influenza. "Oh, the poor man. He died in the camp."

Molly stared at the entry, her fingers tapping on the tablecloth. "Hmm." She picked up Laura's phone, which still displayed Agnes's website. "Okay. There's something odd here. Isabel had a daughter, born in 1944, in Glasgow. That's a very long pregnancy."

"Maybe she got remarried," Carol said.

"I don't think so, unless she found a man with the same last name." Molly handed the phone around. The caption under a cute picture of a small girl behind the bakery counter said, *Sophia Rico serves a customer circa 1950.*

"The scandal could be why she moved to Glasgow," Laura suggested. "She could start a new life there as a widow with a child."

"I suppose you're right," Carol said slowly. "The question is, who was Sophia's father?"

"That certainly is the question." Laura opened a new browser on her phone and began searching for anything to do with Agnes. A number of results came up, including an image she recognized—the old logo, which had been on the business card Charlotte saved. But why?

She recalled that the card had listed an Edinburgh address. Had Charlotte met Agnes in Edinburgh? She looked up Charlotte and dove into details about her work history. Almost two years ago, the actress had worked on a show that filmed in Edinburgh. In the same studios where Agnes started her cooking show.

"Find anything?" Carol asked.

"I'm not sure," Laura said. "I think Charlotte and Agnes knew each other professionally. That's why Charlotte had the old card."

"That makes sense," Molly said. "But does it mean anything?"

Laura pushed back her chair. "Why don't we go ask her?"

The sun was close to the horizon when they reached the path along the loch, and Laura was glad they hadn't lingered in the village any later. Purple and pink clouds drifted in a pale blue sky over the western hills, truly a beautiful sight.

A huddled figure sat on a rock at the height of land above where Charlotte had been found. Molly, who was in the lead, stopped. "Who is it?" she whispered.

Laura recognized the hat. "It's Kyla." She gave Molly a gentle push, an indication to keep walking.

The actress watched them as they approached, her face shadowed by the hat brim. "Nice evening, isn't it?" Although her words were casual, her posture tensed, as though she was poised to flee.

"It is." Laura moved to stand beside Kyla. Carol and Molly went to her other side, standing facing the view. Assuming Kyla had seen them at dinner, Laura said, "Great food at the pub. And then we had tablet at the tearoom."

"Oh, tablet is my favorite," Kyla said, then her voice sharpened. "I overheard you talking to the landlord."

Laura's heart sank. She had been afraid of that. Possible responses flitted through her mind, but she couldn't settle on any of them.

Of course Kyla didn't like the idea that they were asking questions about her movements. Who would?

"All those questions about the night Charlotte died." Kyla stared across the loch. "I was with her, you know. Right here in this spot."

19

Laura froze, afraid a sudden movement might spook the actress. A quick glance at her friends confirmed they were equally enthralled.

Kyla absently played with her skirt, pleating and smoothing the fabric. "I guess it was after Finn left, because she was a mess. I was pretty mad at her. About a bunch of things, honestly. Mostly the way she treated my brother. He was so in love with her." Kyla made a strangled sound. "She really hurt him. And she snatched the limelight away from me every chance she got." Her eyes narrowed. "Get this. *I* was the one who suggested she audition for the show. No good deed, right?"

She fell silent and focused on her skirt. Laura didn't dare to comment, not wanting to break the spell that seemed to have fallen over Kyla. Maybe she didn't have anyone else to confide in about her troubled friendship.

Was she about to confess to murder? Laura's heart lodged in her throat.

"Then she jumped ship. Do you believe it?" Kyla's voice rose with each word. "After all I did for her. After Clive gave her the starring role *and* a raise." She half rose from the rock then settled down again. "Clive's a fool, with an ego so big it blinds him. He didn't believe me when I told him she was leaving. I warned him to rewrite the end of the season to accommodate her departure, but he didn't listen."

"That must have been so frustrating," Carol murmured. Her tone was soothing, understanding, encouraging. Laura imagined her counseling troubled teenagers with that voice.

"It was. Totally." Kyla inhaled a ragged breath. "Finally, I'd had enough. She had already done her worst, so why should I keep quiet? She needed to hear about the effect she had on people. You can't just wreck people's lives and get away with it."

"No, there's always a price to pay," Carol said.

"So there is." Kyla sighed. "And I guess she paid it." She barked a laugh. "But not by my hand. We had a knockdown, drag-out fight, but we were both still standing when I left."

A breath whooshed out of Laura. "She was okay when you left her?"

Kyla's head snapped around, eyes flashing. "What, you actually thought I killed her?"

Carol stepped in with her calming presence. "Of course not. But tell us, Kyla. Did you see anyone else that night?"

The actress rose, twitching her skirt into place. "Yes. That strange little man. The gardener. He was walking along the trail." She shuddered. "I'm so glad he didn't decide to strangle me." With that, she spun on her heel and stalked away.

The women waited on the promontory until Kyla was out of sight up the path. Laura sank down onto the rock the actress had vacated. "I can't believe it. We're back where we started."

"Not quite," Carol said. "I'm not surprised she saw Terry on the path, since he goes that way to get to his cottage."

"A case of wrong place, wrong time," Laura said. "And of course, his scarf was used."

"He makes a good scapegoat," Molly said. "Whoever did it probably didn't bank on Lady Freya hiring a good solicitor."

"They didn't bank on us either." Carol put her hands on her hips. "Let's go, girls. The night is young."

The trio hurried the rest of the way to the castle, conscious of the waning light. They found Lady Freya in the lobby, working behind the desk with Minnie at her feet.

"The others are watching television in the lounge if you'd care to join them," her ladyship said.

"Not right now," Carol said. "But maybe later. Is Agnes around?"

"I believe she's up in her room." Lady Freya frowned. "She said she had a touch of something. I do hope she'll be able to teach tomorrow."

"I hope so too," Laura said, wondering if Agnes caught a bug from the new students. "Which room is she in? We won't bother her if she's sleeping," she added hastily.

Mrs. Beasley entered the lobby, bearing a tea tray. She set it on the counter and began to unload. "Is there anything else, your ladyship? I put snacks and drinks in the lounge for the guests." She regarded the Americans with curiosity.

"No, that's it for tonight, Mrs. Beasley. You can go on home. It's been a long day." As the cook shuffled from the room, Lady Freya said, "Agnes is in the room across the hall from Laura's."

"Simple enough," Carol said. "Thanks." They headed toward the staircase with Minnie lumbering along behind them.

In the upper hall, Molly pressed her ear to Agnes's door. "It's quiet in there," she murmured. "Maybe she's sleeping."

Laura bit her lip. They really needed to speak to Agnes, and the sooner the better. "Let's knock softly a couple of times. If she's awake, she'll hear it."

"Okay," Molly said. "Here goes." She tapped on the door with her knuckles, and to their surprise, it opened. "That's strange. Who leaves their door unlatched like that?"

"What now?" Carol asked. "Should we go in and check on her?"

Minnie took the decision out of their hands. With a butt of her big head, she pushed through the door and trotted inside. The room was in pitch darkness, the heavy curtains drawn.

"Agnes?" Molly called softly. No answer. "I don't think she's in here."

"We should make sure," Laura said, stepping into the room and feeling along the wall for the light switch. The overhead chandelier flared to life.

"Is that Agnes?" Carol pointed to a heap on the bathroom floor, which was also in darkness. The three women rushed to the bathroom, but when Carol switched on that light, they saw it was merely an empty bathrobe.

"Whew," Molly said, her hand on her chest. "That had me worried."

"She's not here." Laura's gaze swept the bathroom and the adjacent bedchamber. "We'd better leave before she comes back and finds us snooping."

"You're right about that." With a laugh, Carol snapped off the bathroom light.

As they walked out, Laura noticed a photograph in a silver frame on the bedside table. Curious, she picked it up, recognizing Agnes's grandmother, who was holding an adorable infant with plump cheeks and a double chin.

"What's that?" Molly came to Laura's side and peeked at the photograph. "Oh, what a cute baby."

"Does she look like someone?" Laura asked.

Carol had now joined them. "The baron. She has his chins."

The women laughed, then Molly peered closer. "I think she has more than his chins. Do you think the baron and Agnes's grandmother…?"

"That may be, but let's talk about it somewhere else. We'd better go." Laura made sure to set the frame exactly where it had been, then headed for the door. Partway there, she stopped. "Where's Minnie?"

"I don't know," Molly said.

"Minnie," Laura called. The dog yipped in response, but Laura still didn't see her. "Where did that come from?"

"I think she's in here." Molly stepped inside the walk-in closet. A moment later, she gasped. "Oh, you've got to see this."

Carol and Laura crowded behind Molly in the closet doorway. In the back of the enclosure was an opening. Another secret door. Somewhere in the passage, Minnie yipped again.

"We'd better get her out of there," Laura said. "Who knows where it goes?" She called for the dog again, and Carol whistled. But Minnie refused to come back out.

Molly groaned. "We can't leave her in there. What if she's trapped?"

Carol switched on her cell phone light and quoted Shakespeare. "'Once more unto the breach, dear friends.'"

"*Macbeth* would be more appropriate, location-wise, but *Henry V* will do," Laura said with a grin, glad that the moment's tension had been broken.

Laura and Molly also switched on their phone lights before they stepped into the secret passage. The thin beams of light revealed Minnie a distance away, down a narrow corridor festooned with cobwebs on the ceiling. Alongside paw prints, scuffs in the dust coating the floor indicated that someone else had come this way recently.

"I wonder if Agnes is exploring the secret passage right now." Laura brought up a picture of the castle map in her mind. "I think you can get to some tunnels this way. Maybe Minnie wants us to find Agnes."

"Or maybe she slipped out of the castle, letting everyone think she was in her bedroom." Molly shone her light into a crevice in the brick wall. "I keep thinking we're going to see a mouse."

"Minnie will scare off any mice," Laura reassured her friend.

Carol stopped short, causing the other two to nearly collide with her back. "She's going down a set of stairs now. Shall we risk it?"

"Absolutely," Laura said. "It's either that or retrace our steps."

The stairs wound down in a similar configuration to the ones leading off Laura's room. Minnie stopped at the bottom of the steps and barked three times. Something scrabbled on the other side of the wall, and the door swung open, revealing a visibly startled Lord Alan.

Despite his surprise, he stood back with a sweeping bow. "Come in, ladies. How good of you to join me." The dog sauntered out of the enclosure, hind end wagging. The women followed, emerging into the castle library.

"Have you been exploring the inner workings of the castle?" Lord Alan asked. "It's fascinating, isn't it?" He moved back to a long table where his papers and books were laid out. They had interrupted his work.

Laura considered how to answer his question. The simple truth was the best option, she decided. "Minnie led us here. We tried to get her to come out of the passage, but she refused."

Lord Alan laughed as he patted Minnie's head. "She's a stubborn one, she is." He rubbed her chin. "What are you up to, girl?" He glanced up at the women. "Which entrance did you use?"

Again Laura decided on the truth. She gave the room number. "We reached it through the walk-in closet. The door to the passage was open."

Lord Alan raised a brow in surprise. "But that's Agnes McVie's room. Where is she? Still upstairs? Freya told me she was ill."

"No, she isn't there," Laura said. "We went to visit her and found the door slightly open. Minnie barged in and when we followed to retrieve her, we discovered the passage was open."

"I wonder where . . ." Lord Alan glanced at the secret door, his words trailing off. Then he squared his shoulders. "I do hope she turns up soon. We don't need our guests getting lost inside the castle walls."

"There wasn't any sign of her in the passage." Laura hoped Agnes wasn't hurt somewhere. "And Minnie did lead us down here."

"I just got here a few minutes ago," Lord Alan said. "She must have come through earlier." He picked up a cell phone. "Let me check with Freya."

Having spent most of the last few decades living in a tiny NYC apartment, Laura hid a smile at the idea of Lord Alan calling his wife inside his own home. Granted, the place was too large to search for people on foot.

The call was short. "Lady Freya said that Agnes sent a text to let her know she was out walking." Lord Alan pretended to wipe his forehead. "Phew. I've been trying to reach Sebastian but he's not answering." He raised an eyebrow above his glasses. "I understand you three saved his life today."

Laura shrugged. "That's a bit of an exaggeration. When we arrived for tea, we found him lying on the floor. Someone attacked him right before we got there."

"He had a head wound," Carol said. "But fortunately it wasn't serious."

His lordship fiddled with his pen. "Very strange. I have no idea who would do such a thing. An attempted robbery, was it?"

"He didn't say anything about a robbery," Molly said. "And neither did the constable."

Laura debated whether to confide their theory to Lord Alan. Maybe he could help them, with his vast knowledge of Glenellen history. "We think it has something to do with his property," she said. "Perhaps someone trying to get their hands on it prematurely."

"But Sebastian doesn't have any heirs," Lord Alan said, sounding astonished. "His uncle died without issue. Sebastian is the last of his line, unfortunately. So sad."

"That's what everyone thought," Laura said. "But we believe Charlotte Martin was descended from his uncle. And so did she."

"Charlotte?" Lord Alan rubbed his chin. "You mean her screenplay was autobiographical?"

"Sort of," Laura said. "The screenplay is a bit more dramatic, but yes. Lord Malcolm secretly married a French woman, then he was reported missing in action. His wife had a baby. Charlotte's grandmother."

"A truly amazing story," Lord Alan said. "How did you figure this out?"

"Lady Isla MacVail's portrait," Laura said. "And some research. The sad thing is, Lord Sebastian was happy to connect with Charlotte."

"A real tragedy," Lord Alan mused. "I'm sorrier than ever about her untimely death."

"Now we're worried about Lord Sebastian," Carol said, urgency in her tone. "We'd better hurry over to the manor and make sure he's still in good health."

Lord Alan insisted on driving them to the manor in his old Land Rover. Minnie came with them as well, riding in the back. The vehicle was battered and splashed with mud, but it had a powerful engine. Within a matter of minutes, they were pulling into the manor drive. As before, lights streamed from many windows on the first floor, giving the building a cheery appearance.

"That car belongs to Sebastian," Lord Alan said, pointing to a Volvo. "It appears that he's home."

The foursome climbed out, accompanied by Minnie, and went to the front door. But once again, the laird didn't answer the bell or knocks on the door.

"Maybe he's in bed," Molly said, though she didn't sound convinced.

"I doubt it," Carol replied. "He doesn't seem the type to leave all the lights on."

"No, Sebastian is a frugal sort," Lord Alan said. "Something is wrong. And in light of his head injury and what you told me, I think entering the house is justified."

Edging past Minnie, who was waiting impatiently to enter, Laura tried to turn the door handle. "It's locked."

"No problem." Lord Alan moved a pot of geraniums. "He's told me where to find the spare key." He displayed a brass key with triumph before unlocking the front door.

Calling for his lordship, they moved through the rooms on the first floor, finding no trace of the homeowner.

"I'll check upstairs," Lord Alan said. He nimbly climbed the staircase only to rejoin the women a short time later. "He's not up there. I'm really getting worried now."

After expecting to find him lying unconscious again, Laura was almost relieved that he wasn't there. But where could he be? She frowned dubiously at Minnie lying on the carpet at the base of the stairs. "Can you find him, Minnie?"

The dog lifted her head and gave a woof, but didn't get up.

"I should have done this before." Lord Alan grabbed the receiver of a landline phone on a table in the entry. "Maybe he ended up hospitalized." But a couple minutes later, he hung up, shaking his head. "He's not there." He thought for a moment before dialing another number. "I'll try his cell phone one more time."

"I hear it," Carol said a moment later, trotting down the hall. They all followed, tracing the ringing sound to Lord Sebastian's study. The phone sat under a stack of papers on the desk.

Lord Alan picked up the ringing phone and shut it off. "Obviously something has happened. If he left under his own steam, went off with a friend or such, he wouldn't leave his phone."

Laura's heart sank. Lord Sebastian had vanished.

20

Everyone collapsed into chairs around the study, except Minnie, who snuffled at the carpet. "Now what?" Molly asked. "Should we call the police?"

"And report what, exactly?" Carol frowned. "He's a grown man who doesn't happen to be home." She gestured at the study. "And there doesn't appear to be any sign of foul play."

"But something's wrong," Laura said. "We all know it." She steeled herself before making her next statement, trying to ignore the dread in her stomach from the fact that she was about to accuse her one-time idol of criminal behavior. "I think Agnes has him."

"Agnes McVie?" Lord Alan's mouth dropped open. "The chef? What has she got to do with this?"

Laura sat up a little straighter, hoping to convince Lord Alan by her confidence if not her argument. "We believe it's possible that Agnes is descended from Lord Sebastian's grandfather, Lord Kenneth. Her grandmother was the cook here at the manor during World War II."

Lord Alan shook his head and blinked, as if stunned. "Run that by me again, please. Not one lost-heir story but two? Incredible."

Between the three of them, they detailed what they had learned about Agnes and her grandmother. "We know that a woman can't inherit the title," Laura said. "But it stands to reason that the real prize is this house and all that comes with it."

"And you think Agnes would kill to get her hands on the inheritance?" Lord Alan asked, his voice rising in disbelief.

I think she already did. But Laura kept that to herself for now. "Yes, I believe so," Laura said, shivering a little at being so bold. But what if they were right and delayed too long? Lord Sebastian was in trouble, she knew that much for certain.

"You women astound me," Lord Alan said. "Maybe I should hire you to help me with research. You have a . . . a certain knack."

"Lucky us," Molly murmured.

Minnie had continued to explore the room, pushing her big body behind the curtains and furniture and sniffing every square inch of the floor. Now she stood at a panel next to the fireplace and howled, then she lifted a massive paw and scuffed at the wood.

"Lord Alan, you told me about the tunnels under the castle grounds," Laura said. "Do tunnels go under this property too?"

He nodded. "They go all the way down to the loch, for ease of commerce, naturally. The interests of the manor house and castle have often been closely aligned. Sebastian is a member of the Cameron clan, you know." He smiled. "He's even more of a believer in the Jacobite gold than I. He told me he's tried to find it by exploring the tunnels. I told him that it was a very dangerous and foolish pursuit." He shrugged. "Not that he'd listen to me."

Laura rose to her feet. "I think I know where to find Lord Sebastian then. And judging by Minnie's behavior, I think she does too."

Lord Alan had more experience with secret compartments, so they let him work on figuring this one out. He finally pressed a molding under the fireplace mantel and a piece of the paneling slid open, releasing a gust of dank air. Minnie tried to bolt inside but Lord Alan grabbed her collar. "Hold your horses, old girl. I don't want you getting lost." With a grumble, the dog plopped in front of the fireplace.

"We need better flashlights than this," Carol said, waving her phone. "And forgive me, but do you have any idea where we're going, Lord Alan?"

The laird drew himself upright. "Those are both good points. Let me have Lady Freya e-mail me the tunnel map for this part of Glenellen." He pulled out his smartphone and placed the call. "Hello, dear. I have a request. Now before I tell you, you have to promise not to get angry."

Laura waved her hand, interrupting. "And have her call the police if we don't return within a certain amount of time."

He put up a finger. "Yet another good point. Our American guests are really quite brilliant, Freya. You already knew that? Why am I not surprised? Always ahead of me, you are." He relayed the request to notify the police, which resulted in much squawking on the other end. "Now, don't fret, dear. I'm sure it won't be necessary. It's merely a precaution. I have to go—they're waiting on me." He quickly hung up and faced the women, who were smiling in spite of themselves.

"It sounds like that went over well," Carol said mildly.

Lord Alan ducked his head with a sheepish grin. "She promised to send the tunnel map immediately. She also said that Sebastian keeps torches in the broom closet."

"'Torch' is what they call a flashlight," Molly whispered helpfully to the others.

"I'll go check," Carol said.

"And I'll see what else we can find that might come in useful," Molly added.

The pair hurried off while Laura and Lord Alan waited for the e-mail to come through, which took about ten seconds. "We really do have great service," he muttered. "Before we moved, I was afraid we wouldn't—" His fingers flew over the screen. "Take a look at this, Laura."

Laura stared at the map, noticing that the underground route in question was simple, just one main corridor straight from the manor to the loch with two side branches that went to the village and the castle. She closed her eyes, seeing the map in her mind.

"I'll bring this with us," Lord Alan said, tucking the phone into his pocket. "But yes, it's good to memorize what you can."

Carol and Molly burst back into the room, arms full. "Here you go," Carol said, handing Laura and Lord Alan each a flashlight. "We found a battery-powered lantern too. I'll carry that." She set it on the desk for now.

"And we also brought clothesline." Molly showed them the bundle. "And a knife." She pushed the sheathed knife through her belt. "Masking tape, a first aid kit, and bottled water. Plus a pack of biscuits." All these items were split between two carryalls. Molly slung one over her shoulder and Laura took the other.

"We were all scouts as girls," Laura explained, seeing Lord Alan's amazement.

He nodded in approval. "Well done. Shall we start?" Using his phone, he took a photo of the opening in the wall and sent a text. "A time stamp for Freya. The clock is now ticking."

Minnie went first, followed by Lord Alan, Carol, and Molly, with Laura bringing up the rear. This passageway was very similar to the one in the castle, Laura noticed. *Right down to the cobwebs.*

After a short distance, they descended a set of steps. Here, another door barred their way.

"This was so the king's men or any other enemies couldn't find the tunnels," Lord Alan said. "People escaped from the manor this way. Or brought in goods that escaped taxes." He soon found a hidden latch, and the door swung forward. "We'll leave it open." He used a piece of timber to prop the door in place.

"Good idea," Carol said. "I don't relish the idea of getting stuck."

Laura's chest tightened as they entered the tunnel, which was wider than the secret passage but had a fairly low ceiling. She told herself to take deep breaths and relax. It was just another adventure.

They weren't going to be trapped underground, not with Lord Alan and Minnie as guides.

While they made their way deeper into the tunnel, Laura tried to picture where they were. The land sloped down to the loch, so the tunnel did as well. At the other end, it must be hewn from rock, bored right through the cliffs. How did men do that in an era when they lacked power tools?

"Smell that?" Carol asked. "Sea air."

"Is that a good thing?" Laura breathed deeply, the coolness soothing her nerves slightly.

"Absolutely," Lord Alan said. "It means it's still open all the way. One of the castle tunnels is blocked by a collapse. The timbers gave way." He laughed. "With my luck, the Jacobite gold is probably under the rubble."

Laura grimaced, imagining a tunnel failure, the creak and groan of ancient timbers breaking, the thunder of tons of rocks and soil burying everything. *Burying us.* She used her flashlight to study the ceiling. The wood appeared perfectly fine, as did the bricks reinforcing the walls.

Reviewing the map in her mind, she wondered when they would come across the branches leading to the village and to the castle. What if Agnes and Lord Sebastian were down one of those? What if they weren't in the tunnels at all? Did Agnes have a vehicle? She kicked herself for not even asking.

"Lord Alan," she called. "Did Agnes drive herself to the castle?"

He paused, as did Carol and Molly, and he glanced back at Laura. "Let me think." After a few beats, he said, "No, she arrived by train. Took a hired car from the station."

"I see where you're going with that," Carol said. "They might not even be down here." Her shoulders sagged.

"I have a feeling they are," Molly said. "And so does Minnie."

At the mention of her name, the dog whined. She pawed at the dirt floor as though eager to keep going.

Relief lifted Laura's spirits. "I think she's picked up Lord Sebastian's scent."

Lord Alan patted Minnie's head. "You're a very good dog, aren't you? Go on, Minnie, find Sebastian." As they began walking again, he said, "She likes Sebastian. He'll play fetch with her for hours."

Maybe that was why Minnie had brought the scrap of tartan to the manor—as a present for her friend. Only she'd decided the Americans needed it more.

They trudged on along the tunnel, and Laura started to feel as if they were never going to find the end. Or Lord Sebastian.

Finally, they reached an opening to the left, an oval cut into the wall. Lord Alan stopped. "That tunnel goes all the way to the village," he said. "Some of the smuggled goods went that way for distribution, I'm sure."

"Do people still use it?" Carol asked.

Lord Alan shook his head. "When they reconstructed the road into the village, they blocked the entrance. It was a huge debate at the time, but in the end, the new road won."

"That means Agnes and Lord Sebastian probably didn't go that way then," Laura said, glad to eliminate a possibility.

"No reason to," Lord Alan agreed, moving on.

The tunnel to the castle appeared soon after. "It gets complicated in there," Lord Alan said. "There's a second route to the loch and a couple of branches. My ancestors were tunnel crazy, it seems."

A short distance later, Laura's toe scuffed something in the dirt. It flew through the air and hit the bricks with a clink. Curious, she bent to pick it up. It was a circular object, crusted with filth. But as she scratched at it, a hint of yellow appeared.

Is it a coin? Laura glanced up to call to her companions, but they were already a distance away, their lights bobbing in the dark. She tucked it into her pocket, but before she took a step, a strange sound caught her ear.

Instinct made her leap aside in time to avoid a figure rushing at her. It was Mrs. Beasley, face twisted in anger, arms outstretched. Thanks to Laura's side step, the cook went sailing past her and stumbled into a wall. She straightened with a growl, hands curled like claws.

"I wouldn't, if I were you." Laura raised her long, heavy flashlight defensively. "What are you doing down here?"

Mrs. Beasley backed away. "Just helping a friend." Her gaze sharpened. "What did you find? I saw you pick something up."

"Nothing," Laura said. "I dropped a quarter out of my pocket. A quarter is one of our American coins."

"I know what it is," the cook snarled.

The lights stopped up ahead. "Laura, where are you?" Carol called, and Minnie woofed in concern.

"I'm right here," Laura replied.

"Don't say a word about me," Mrs. Beasley ordered, then melted back into the shadows.

Of course Laura didn't obey. As soon as she caught up with the others, she told them, "Mrs. Beasley is skulking around the tunnels. I think she's in cahoots with Agnes." Laura had to admit she enjoyed using the words *skulk* and *cahoots*, which she didn't usually have reason to use. Exploring tunnels in Scotland was certainly well outside the ordinary.

"We saw Mrs. Beasley talking to Agnes in the kitchen, remember?" Molly raised her eyebrows. "I bet it was about more than baking."

Lord Alan snorted in disbelief. "I'm sorry, ladies, but I can't believe that Mrs. Beasley, of all people, is up to no good. She's worked for our family for decades."

"Can you think of a good reason why she's down here in the tunnels?" Laura asked. "Maybe she was looking for things like this." She dug the artifact out of her pocket and held it out, spotlighting it with her flashlight.

"Oh my." Lord Alan picked up the object and scraped at it with a fingernail. "This looks like a gold coin."

Laura's heart leaped. "Jacobite gold?" And to think she had merely stumbled on it after people had hunted for centuries.

"Maybe." Lord Alan held it up. "Mind if I keep it?"

"Of course not," Laura said. "It belongs to you or Lord Sebastian. But promise me you'll let us know what it turns out to be."

"Promise." Lord Alan buttoned the find inside the breast pocket of his tweed jacket. "Onward. Not much farther now."

Sticking close to the others and remaining vigilant for another attack by Mrs. Beasley, Laura focused on the goal—reaching the end of this dark, cramped space.

The brick walls soon became stone, a sign that they had reached the cliffs. The sound of water lapping against rocks drifted to their ears, another indication they were close to the loch.

Lord Alan put a finger to his lips. "We're almost to the cave. Be extra quiet from now on as sounds tend to echo." Even Minnie seemed to quiet her panting.

The fresh air grew stronger, as did the gurgle of water. The ceiling lifted and rounded. Underfoot, the packed dirt became sand. They had reached the cave.

"You don't have a choice." These menacing words from Agnes McVie proved the truth of Lord Alan's warning about sound traveling. They couldn't see Agnes, but her words were clear.

"Douse most of the lights," Lord Alan whispered. "We need to get the lay of the land."

Leaving only a phone flashlight on, they crept forward again. Laura winced at an occasional crunch from a shoe. But what could they do? They had to find out what Agnes was up to. After rounding an outcropping, Lord Alan gave the signal to turn on the lights. He stabbed a finger to where a figure stood in the gloom.

The lights flared to life, illuminating a terrible scene. Silhouetted against a large opening and the glossy black loch beyond, Agnes loomed menacingly over Lord Sebastian, holding a dangerously large rock above his head.

"Halt right there." Lord Alan's voice barked with the authority of many noble generations. "Put that stone down."

Lord Sebastian lifted his head a little. "Alan. Thank goodness." In the light, Laura saw his head wound was bleeding again.

"Stay back or I'll kill him," Agnes said, then gave a mocking laugh. "How sad for the last laird of the manor to die while searching for gold. Say hello to the new lady of the manor." She glared down at Lord Sebastian. "You never should have had the property. As the daughter of Lord Kenneth, the man who took advantage of my poor grandmother, my mother should have been the rightful heir."

She's entirely off base, Laura thought fleetingly as Agnes continued to rant about how she should have "finished the job" on Sebastian earlier that day. *Even if her mother had been legitimate, Sophia would have been third in line behind Archibald and Malcolm. If anything, Charlotte was the rightful heir as a descendant of Kenneth's oldest son.*

Shelving the ancestry calculations with a mental shake, Laura steeled herself to take action and glanced toward her friends.

Apparently sharing Laura's readiness, Molly dropped her voice to the slightest whisper. "On the count of three, Carol, shine your light in her eyes. Laura, help me jump her."

Laura and Carol gave tiny nods of agreement. Rather than count out loud, Molly used her foot to tap beats. On three, Carol shone the big flashlight right into Agnes's face and the other two burst into action. They sprinted the short distance and leaped upon the other woman, pushing her well away from Lord Sebastian. Minnie helped, using her big paws to knock Agnes backward.

Agnes dropped the rock but fought like a wildcat. Laura tried to corral the woman's thrashing limbs. Minnie barked, a thunderous sound in the cave. Behind them, Laura was dimly aware of Lord Alan hurrying to his friend's side. Then another figure burst out of the darkness and jumped onto Laura's back.

She recognized the growling in her ear. Mrs. Beasley was back again.

"Give it up!" Laura yelled, struggling to push the woman off her. "You're outnumbered." Finally, Laura's flailing elbow connected with Mrs. Beasley's stomach, making her stagger backward with a grunt. Minnie leaped up and grabbed the woman's skirt in her teeth. It tore with a loud rip.

Carol had now joined Molly, and between the two of them, they pinned Agnes down. The baking star continued to thrash, forcing them to sit on her legs and wind the clothesline they'd brought along around her ankles. Lord Alan staunched Lord Sebastian's bleeding with a handkerchief, using the other hand to make a call. "The authorities are on their way," he announced a few moments later.

Mrs. Beasley leaped to her feet and dashed from the cave in response, but Laura didn't chase her. The police would certainly apprehend her at the tunnel's entrance.

"You might as well stop struggling," Laura said to Agnes. "It's all over." *Including your career—and any lingering hero worship I had for you.*

Lord Sebastian was sitting up now, his face pale and his clothing quite rumpled, but apparently otherwise all right. "You know what is so sad about this? I would have welcomed an heir or two."

Agnes responded with a snarl. "Tell that to my grandmother, turned out onto the streets without a shilling and with a mouth to feed. My mother deserved to inherit the estate more than you did."

Times had changed, but humankind had not, Laura reflected. Some people were still selfish and greedy. But watching Lord Alan tenderly check his friend's wound, she knew they could also be loving and kind.

"Hold still, old boy," Lord Alan said. "Help is on its way."

The rumble of boat engines and flashing lights announced the arrival of the police via the loch. After an initial examination, Lord Sebastian was gently loaded onto one watercraft, which sped him away to the hospital.

As Agnes was arrested, Laura heard her babbling a confession, though it didn't sound entirely truthful. "Charlotte's death was an accident, okay? We had an argument about our inheritance rights and it got physical. In the struggle, she fell over the cliff. I didn't know she was so close to the edge."

"And the scarf that strangled her?" Inspector Gough asked, his tone stern.

The baker's mouth flapped as she sputtered, caught in a lie about how Charlotte had died. Then her shoulders sagged. "All right, I stole it. And used Kyla's cloak as a disguise. Otherwise Charlotte wouldn't have talked to me. But I didn't plan to kill her. It just happened."

Laura didn't think strangulations happened on accident. But that was up to the jury to decide, she supposed, though she had a good idea which way they would go.

A short time later, Detective Inspector Wilson escorted Agnes to the police boat. While the craft zoomed away, lights flashing, Inspector Gough and Constable Hail trudged across the sand to Lord Alan and the three friends.

"We'd like complete statements from you all," the inspector said. "But we can do that somewhere more comfortable."

"I suggest we go to the castle," Lord Alan said. "I'll have Lady Freya put on the kettle." He sent a quick text.

Laura groaned, not wanting to travel through the tunnel again. "Is there another way to get there?"

"Oh yes," Lord Alan said to her relief. "Outside the cave, there is a staircase built into the cliff. It's the shortest way and it's sturdy. We make sure of that with regular maintenance." He reached out and patted Minnie. "But I'll have to take this old girl along the shore. I think she's too tired for that many stairs after all the other excitement today. I know I am."

After the inspector said a few words to a team collecting evidence in the now brightly lit cave, the small group made their way out to the open air. As the laird had promised, a metal staircase with handrails zigzagged up the rock face.

"We're getting a workout tonight," Carol said, regarding the stairs. "Oh well, up we go."

Soon the straggling, tired band arrived at the castle, meeting up with Lord Alan and Minnie on the path. They entered the dining room through the terrace entrance, where urns of hot water and coffee awaited, along with plates of sandwiches and biscuits.

Lady Freya greeted her husband with an eager embrace, then held him at arm's length. "What on earth is going on, dear?"

"Pour a cup of tea and sit with us," Lord Alan said. "You can hear all about it."

While fortifying themselves with snacks and hot beverages, Laura and her friends gave statements about the evening's events, starting with going to Agnes's room and finding the chef missing.

"I think Mrs. Beasley overheard us talking to you, Lady Freya," Laura said. "She stalked us down the tunnel and showed up in the cave when we were fighting with Agnes."

Lady Freya gasped. "Irma Beasley did that?" A series of expressions flitted over her face, ending with a nod of understanding. "Now a lot of things make sense. She said something about her grandmother being great friends with Agnes's."

So the scorned woman had remained in contact with friends after leaving Glenellen, Laura realized, and decades later their granddaughters had tried to exact a terrible revenge.

"Have Irma Beasley picked up for questioning," Inspector Gough said to the constable. After Hail relayed the order into a radio, Laura and the others continued their story. Minnie received her fair share of credit for tracking Agnes and Lord Sebastian to the manor's hidden passage.

"Your dog is amazing," Molly told Lady Freya. "She found some of the most important clues too."

"Like Charlotte's cell phone," Lady Freya said. She patted her pet's large head. "You deserve a special treat today, Minnie." She opened a tin and gave Minnie a dog biscuit. "She loves these, but only gets them on special occasions."

"I think today is certainly that," Lord Alan said.

Laura remembered the tartan strip. "The cell phone wasn't the only clue she found. Hold on—I'll be right back." Before leaving the room, she said to Lady Freya, "Want to get the cloak for the officers? I think it's more relevant now that we know Agnes wore it."

Laura dashed upstairs to retrieve the cloth strip, Charlotte's notebook and screenplay, and *Burke's Peerage*. By the time she got back, the damaged cloak was spread out on a table, and everyone was gathered around it. Laura placed the plastic bag with the missing strip in the correct location to show that it matched.

"In addition to all this," Laura said, showing them Charlotte's documents, "Agnes has a photograph of her mother that greatly resembles the old baron. It's in her room." The star baker's bedchamber was now sealed off, so Laura hadn't gone in. "Pictures of the baron can be found at The Library Tearoom, along with some of Agnes's grandmother."

The officers exchanged glances. "Impressive," the inspector muttered. "What did you say you do in the States?"

"We run a bakehouse," Molly said with a laugh. "But I guess we have other talents."

"I'll say," Constable Hail said with admiration. "Maybe I should take lessons from you ladies." Her enthusiasm wilted under Inspector Gough's reproving glare. "Not that we don't get good training."

"Of course you do," Lady Freya said genially. "Now who wants another cup of tea?"

The next afternoon, Lord Sebastian answered the manor doorbell sporting a bandage around his head. "Do come in, ladies. Tea is waiting on the terrace." The previous night, Lord Sebastian had been treated and released from the hospital. This visit was to make up for the meal interrupted by the first attack on him.

"Thank you for the invitation," Laura said. "We brought along some Montrose tea cakes we made this morning." A floral scent wafted across the air as she opened the tin container to show him the tiny cakes speckled with dried fruit. Rose water was one of the ingredients, which had always charmed Laura.

"Una from The Library Tearoom took over the lessons for Agnes," Carol explained as they entered the manor. "She's just as skilled, even if she's less famous."

"You mean notorious," Lord Sebastian said, a hand going to his bandage. He was right about that. According to Molly, the story was being blasted around the world through the tabloids, news channels, and social media. Agnes's show had been canceled, though interest in *A Highland Lass* was soaring.

"We still have a few more days here, fortunately," Molly said. "Maybe we'll be able to relax and focus on our baking."

"I'm more relaxed already," Laura put in with a laugh. "And last night I slept great." With Agnes and Mrs. Beasley both under arrest, Laura no longer feared intruders sneaking into her room through the secret door. They'd come to learn that the cook had helped Agnes after being promised a job at the manor with much less work and a lot more pay.

The group had barely settled into lovely wicker furniture on the terrace when the doorbell rang again. Lord Sebastian started to get up. "I have no idea who that is," he said. "I'm not expecting any other visitors."

"Please sit. I'll go," Laura said, since she was closest. She hurried through the house as the bell chimed again.

A young woman with raven hair stood in the front portico, an uncertain expression on her face. "Does Lord Sebastian MacVail live here?" she asked, her voice bearing a French accent. "The nice woman at the castle sent me over. I do hope I have the right place."

"He certainly does," Laura said, thinking something about the woman's features seemed familiar.

A brief, almost scared smile flitted across the woman's face. "Can you please tell him that Monique Martin is here? Charlotte is—was my sister." Grief shadowed her eyes at the mention of the actress.

But a rush of joy flooded Laura when she realized the implications of Monique's visit. Here was the heir Lord Sebastian longed for. "Come in," she said. "I know he'll be very happy to see you."

Out on the terrace, introductions were made as Monique took a seat, though no one mentioned the young lady's familial ties to their host.

"I own a small flower shop in France," Monique said in response to questions about where she lived. "In a tiny little village in the middle of nowhere. I keep what you call a low profile. I asked Charlotte not to mention me." Tears filled her expressive eyes. "And she didn't. Not once."

"That's true," Molly said. "I've read a lot of her interviews, and she didn't discuss any family."

Lord Sebastian pulled out a snowy handkerchief and handed it to the young woman. While she dabbed at her eyes, he asked, "Did she say anything about what she sought here in Glenellen?"

Monique looked at him with curiosity. "She only told me that it was the filming location for the show. I had to come and see it when I found out she died here. It felt like the last way I could connect with my sister. And from what I've seen, it was a perfect choice as a filming location. The castle, the hills, the loch—all very historic and beautiful."

The laird drew in a breath. "I have some news for you, Mademoiselle Martin. Good news, I think, but bound to be rather startling."

"Monique, please," she murmured, crumpling the handkerchief in her fist. "What is this news? Please tell me."

Lord Sebastian studied his new guest before rising to his feet. "Follow me. I think this discussion is best held inside."

"All right." Monique accepted the hand he extended to help her out of her chair.

At the doorway, their host gestured for Laura and the others to come along. "You're part of this story now," he said, standing aside to let them precede him into the drawing room.

Once in the house, he led them all into the small sitting room, where Lord Sebastian put a gentle arm around Monique and led her to the portrait. "This is my ancestor, Lady Isla MacVail."

Monique stared at the painting for a long moment, a hand to her mouth. "She . . . she looks like Charlotte." She squinted. "And me, a little."

"Lady Isla is your ancestor too," Lord MacVail said. "You are my cousin, if a few generations removed. It seems my uncle married your great-grandmother in France before he went missing in action. This was during World War II, mind you. Most of the details are missing."

"I never knew we had relatives." Tears began to stream down Monique's cheeks. "Our parents are gone and now Charlotte . . ." She hugged Lord Sebastian. "I am so thrilled to meet you."

He gazed down into her face. "And I feel the same about you."

In tacit agreement to give the newfound family some space, Laura and her friends quietly slipped from the room. As they headed down to the loch path, having walked over to the manor this time, Carol said, "I think our work here is done."

"Yes, I believe so," Laura said. Nothing could erase the tragedy of Charlotte's death, but at least Monique and Lord Sebastian now had each other. Laura found it interesting that Monique was focused on the relationship, not Lord Sebastian's estate. She was the opposite of Agnes, who had tried to eliminate the relatives standing between her and a fortune.

At the height of land, the three friends linked arms and gazed over the water. "I'm never, ever going to forget this trip," Laura declared. "I'll be thinking about it every time I make one of the recipes we've learned."

"With any luck, you'll be remembering the trip a lot," Molly said. "Our first summer is ahead." Although Loch Mallaig hosted visitors all year, summer was by far the busiest season for the lakeshore town, and the Bakehouse Three had high hopes for a successful season.

Carol took a deep breath of fresh air. "I love it here. But I tell you what—I can't wait to give Harvey his new hat." Laughing merrily, the friends headed along the path toward the castle.

22

Harvey came to meet them right outside the airport security gate—along with an eager companion, Angus. With a fierce scrabbling of claws and a few frantic yips, the Scottish terrier bolted toward his mistress. While onlookers smiled, Molly dropped her carry-on bag and gathered him into her arms. He wriggled and whined, licking her cheeks.

"Cut it out." Molly laughed at her pet's antics. "I'm glad someone missed me."

"We all did." Harvey put an arm around his wife, his affable face beaming. "Loch Mallaig was a lonely place without you three to liven things up."

Laura exchanged smiles with Carol and Molly. Wherever they went, excitement did seem to follow.

Next they stopped at baggage claim to retrieve their large suitcases, and then carted everything out of the terminal. To Laura's surprise, Fergus MacGregor was waiting in the short-term parking area, standing beside one of the passenger vans from his resort, Castleglen. The back doors were open, ready for their luggage.

"Fergus." Molly stopped dead, but Angus strained ahead on his leash, eager to say hello. "I had no idea you were coming to greet us."

Laura and Carol exchanged glances, amused by their friend's reaction to the handsome resort owner's presence.

"He suggested using the van," Harvey said, opening the side door. "I thought that was a good idea. There's a lot more room, and we figured we'd need it with all the souvenirs you'd probably bring back."

"It was a nice day for a ride," Fergus said with a laugh. "But the real reason is that it's great to have you all home." He gave each woman a hug of greeting, lingering the longest with Molly, or so it seemed to Laura. After releasing her, he grabbed the suitcases and stowed them in the rear while everyone else piled into the van.

"All set?" Fergus asked as he climbed in and started the engine.

Before getting into the passenger seat, Harvey held up a cardboard carrier with to-go cups in it that had been resting there. "We picked up coffees on the way. Thought you might need a little pick-me-up after that flight."

"Bless you, Harvey," Laura said, accepting a cup eagerly.

Carol beamed at her husband. "I knew I married you for a reason."

As Fergus pulled away from the terminal and merged onto the highway, everyone settled in for the ride, sipping coffee and watching the passing scenery. Urban concrete soon gave way to green countryside. Spring had advanced while they were gone, with trees in full leaf and flower beds blooming.

Laura's heart beat faster as they drove along the now familiar road to Loch Mallaig. They were almost home.

Bread on Arrival, located on Tattie Bogle Road, was the first stop, since Molly and Angus lived in the second-floor apartment above the bakery. The gorgeous yellow Victorian—complete with turret, gables, and gingerbread trim—was a former funeral home, hence the bakehouse's tongue-in-cheek name.

As Molly gathered her things, she paused and smiled at Carol and Laura. "You know what tonight is?"

"No, what?" Laura could think of nothing more pressing than a good night's sleep. She was longing to sleep in her own bed again.

"Another episode of *A Highland Lass*," Molly said. "I think we should all get together and watch it." When she was greeted with groans from Laura and Carol, she added, "We're not open tomorrow. You can sleep all day."

"I'd like to see it, if only to learn what all the fuss is about," Fergus said.

"I'm game if you are, Fergus," Harvey said. He was now sporting the red tartan tam and looked extremely dashing.

"Why don't you all come over here to watch the show?" Molly asked, her eyes bright. "I'll make Scotch pies for dinner. Carol, Laura, bring salad and dessert. Fergus and Harvey, cold drinks."

Harvey's brow furrowed in confusion. "No offense, Molly, but I didn't think you were the baker in the bunch."

"I'm not," Molly admitted. "But I can make a mean Scotch pie. Just ask your wife." She blew on her knuckles then rubbed them on her chest. "I aced the pastry in our class."

"She did," Carol said. "Now let's get you upstairs so the rest of us can get home. I'm dying for a hot shower."

A short while later, after having dropped the MacCallans at their log home, Fergus delivered Laura and her luggage to her cottage, which was close to Castleglen. Laura thanked Fergus and told him she'd see him at the bakehouse that evening, then closed the front door and took a moment to luxuriate in the familiar, comfortable silence her tranquil cottage offered.

A stark contrast to her cramped studio apartment, which had been furnished with more bohemian trappings, the historic crofter's cottage was mostly white with the occasional splash of gray, blue, or soft pink. The bright yet serene scheme reminded her considerably of the home her grandparents had lived in when Laura was young. She and her grandmother had made as many memories as cookies and pies in that kitchen.

Feeling the coffee kick in, Laura unpacked her suitcase and started a load of laundry, then went through her mail and made a grocery list. Molly had asked her to bring dessert that evening, and her mind whirred through the recipes they'd worked on at Glenellen Castle. Which one should she make? With a smile, she settled on sticky toffee pudding, which Una had taught them in the last class.

List in hand, she climbed into her red Volkswagen Beetle convertible, put the top down to let in the sweet spring air, and set off for the local grocery store, The Hamper. She lingered for a moment in the ample Scottish foods section, smiling as she spotted many labels now familiar to her after more than a week in Scotland. She put some sparkling pressé in her cart, then moved along to the dairy case.

As she drove home down Yooper Boulevard, Laura appreciated the deep blue of Loch Mallaig's eponymous lake to one side, then, on the other side, caught sight of Bread on Arrival through the trees of Dumfries Park. On a whim, she decided to take a detour.

Molly had gone in through the side entrance, so the front door of the bakery was still locked. The stained glass design of bread loaves and Celtic knots embedded in the door was just as beautiful as Laura remembered, and it brought a smile to her face as she inserted her key. She stepped into the café area, where everything was as it should be, if a little stuffy from being closed up.

Laura strolled around the large room, enjoying afresh the polished wood floors, stone fireplace, and Northwoods furniture. She pictured it open again, filled with patrons chatting and laughing, lining up at the long counters for their orders.

She loved the bakehouse and adored that it was fast becoming the heart of her adopted community. They had many regulars who stopped in each morning to buy treats and catch up on local news. And lots of tourists also patronized the bakery, which—thanks to Molly's PR skills—had already been featured in tourism write-ups as one of the must-visit places in Loch Mallaig.

Laura entered a short hall, which had restrooms labeled *Lads* and *Lassies* on the right and the kitchen to the left. She pushed through a swinging door into her second home, where she felt just as comfortable as she did at her cottage—if not more so.

She set down her grocery bags, then stood in the middle of the floor. She turned in a slow circle, taking in the commercial ovens and stove, the work counters, the walk-in refrigerator, and the neatly organized shelves of bowls and baking pans. She'd never had a hand in choosing her own professional equipment until opening the bakehouse, and the experience had given her a sense of ownership she hadn't experienced before.

Just then, Molly bustled into the kitchen toting her own bags from The Hamper. "Long time, no see."

Laura laughed. "I couldn't stay away. We must have just missed each other at the store."

As they had all the previous week, Laura and Molly worked side by side on their respective dishes. A while later, they'd both finished their projects and the kitchen was spick-and-span—ready for Laura to get right back into it the following day to restock the now woefully empty display cases out front.

Laura helped Molly cart the pint-size Scotch pies up to her den, where she'd set up a table long enough to accommodate everyone. Once the pies were in place, Laura stood back and admired them, all delicately browned and perfect. "I'm impressed, Molly. Should I be worried about my job?"

Molly laughed. "I don't think so. It was a lot of work, and I only made twelve."

"Good thing," Fergus said from the doorway. "I want two." He glanced behind him to where the MacCallans were arriving on the second-floor landing from the bakery. "How about you, Harvey?"

Still sporting the red plaid tam, Harvey rubbed his belly. "Yes sir, I can eat two." Angus, who had been napping in the bedroom, hurried out to greet the guests. "And maybe I'll even share with my best buddy here."

Someone was knocking at the outside door, and Molly hurried to answer. Laura smiled when she saw that the newcomers were their part-time helper, Hamish Bruce, and his wife, Joyce.

"I invited them last minute," Molly said. "Bridget too. She should be here any moment."

"The more the merrier." Carol smiled in greeting as she set her large garden salad in the center of the table.

Joyce held up a casserole dish with oven mitts. "I made my famous baked beans."

"Yum," Laura said, then turned to Hamish, who was a retired history teacher. "We could have used your expertise in Scotland."

Joyce's brows rose. "With the baking lessons? Surely not."

Laura laughed. "No, we ended up doing some genealogy research and reuniting a long-lost heiress with her cousin, a Scottish nobleman." With that teaser causing Hamish to sputter with curiosity, Laura went to greet the bakehouse's other part-time employee, Bridget Ross, who had just arrived.

"Welcome back," Bridget said. "Molly told me what you were making for dessert, so I brought homemade ice cream to go with it." She hefted a lidded metal bowl.

"Perfect." Laura hugged her in greeting, then took the bowl. "I'll put the ice cream in the freezer. You go ahead into the den."

Everyone helped themselves to plates of food, making small talk and catching the bakehouse owners up on local happenings during dinner. Then, once big bowls of toffee pudding and ice cream were dished up, Fergus said, "All right, ladies. Take it from the top."

Laura wasn't sure what Carol had told Harvey, but just about everything would be news to Fergus, Hamish, Joyce, and Bridget. How to begin? Carol and Molly were watching her with expectant expressions.

"Well," Laura said. "The short story is, we helped solve another murder. Not that we planned to. But sadly, Charlotte Martin, the actress, was killed at the castle where we were staying."

Joyce gasped, clutching at Hamish's arm. "Oh my."

"I heard about Charlotte," Bridget said, her face going pale. "But I didn't make the connection to you three. Were you in danger?"

Laura caught her friends' eyes. "At times," she admitted. "But it all worked out."

Between the three of them, they told the entire story, filling the hour until the showing of *A Highland Lass*.

With a few minutes remaining before the show started, Molly stood up and retrieved a bag from a corner of the room. "We have souvenirs for all of you, naturally."

Hamish, Joyce, Fergus, and Bridget loved their gifts. Fergus and Joyce received cream wool scarves, while Hamish got one in Clan Bruce tartan.

Bridget put her earmuffs on immediately. "I'm wearing these everywhere," she declared. "I love them."

"Not at work, I hope," Hamish said.

Bridget sent him a teasing smile. "Only when I have annoying customers." She pulled off the muffs. "Just kidding."

"The show's coming on." Molly grabbed the remote control and aimed it at the television. She found the right channel just in time, and the evocative notes of the opening music drifted through the room—layers of bagpipes, fiddle, whistle, and bodhran. Everyone settled down to watch, soon caught up in the excellent presentation. Seeing Charlotte alive on screen added great poignancy.

"She was so beautiful," Bridget whispered when the show ended. She sat on the rug, knees up to her chin. She brushed away a tear. "It's so sad."

"It is," Laura agreed. "We were thrilled that her sister showed up."

"And now she's the heir, right?" Bridget asked.

Laura nodded. Then a news bulletin scrolling across the screen caught her eye. *Important find in Scottish tunnel. Possible Jacobite gold.*

Molly gave a yelp and pressed a button on the remote, only to change the channel by mistake. With the group's raucous teasing egging her on, she managed to switch it back and increase the volume.

"Some fascinating news from overseas," a news commentator was saying. "This rare gold coin found in an underground tunnel in Scotland might actually be Jacobite gold." In the corner was a picture of the coin, now cleaned and shining. The anchor went on to give some general background about Bonnie Prince Charlie and the doomed uprising.

"Laura found that coin," Carol said. "People have been looking for hundreds of years, and she stumbled across it by accident."

Fergus whistled. "That's amazing."

"The location is not being disclosed until further excavation can be done," the commentator went on. "But the property owners are hopeful that a cache of gold rumored to be lost since the 1700s has finally come to light."

"You seriously found that treasure?" Bridget asked, wide-eyed.

"Tell us more," Joyce encouraged.

Laura looked around the circle of eager faces. "You heard what the man said. This has to stay in this room, okay?" Bridget crossed her heart and the others nodded. Even Angus yipped in agreement. "Well, we were on our way to save Lord Sebastian when . . ."

As Laura told the story to these friends who had become as close to her as family, she couldn't help but think that Lord Alan and Lady Freya could keep their Scottish gold. She had all the treasure she needed right here in Loch Mallaig.